WIGFORD REMEMBERIES

WIGFORD
REMEMBERIES

A NOVEL

KYP HARNESS

NIGHTWOOD EDITIONS

2016

Nightwood Editions
P.O. Box 1779
Gibsons, BC V0N 1V0
Canada
www.nightwoodeditions.com

COVER DESIGN & TYPOGRAPHY: Carleton Wilson

 Canada Council Conseil des Arts
for the Arts du Canada

 BRITISH COLUMBIA
ARTS COUNCIL
An agency of the Province of British Columbia

Nightwood Editions acknowledges financial support from the Government of
Canada through the Canada Book Fund and the Canada Council for the Arts,
and from the Province of British Columbia through the British Columbia
Arts Council and the Book Publisher's Tax Credit.

This book has been produced on 100% post-consumer recycled,
ancient-forest-free paper, processed chlorine-free
and printed with vegetable-based dyes.

Printed and bound in Canada.

CIP data available from Library and Archives Canada.

ISBN 13: 978-0-88971-319-2

ISBN 10: 0-88971-319-7

CONTENTS

❂

WIGFORD REMEMBERIES

GENTLE MIGHTY HANDS

AND NO I NEVER WILL FORGET—NO NO—HOWLING winds, flurries of snow through the grey sky down the gravel sideroad down the hill over the creek up the hill to the little farmhouse with the linoleum floors and an old white stove burning a constant fire over which there was a black iron lid over a hole through which he spat his tobacco and a door opening at the top of the stairs. *Well! Come in, come in!* and *You'll be staying for supper won't you?* with the thermometer and the barometer and the ticking clock and back a while to the house down the old sideroad with the weeds and the ditch and the verdant green forest alongside a creek brown and flowing by the wire fences, oh yes, and foxes and rabbits in the thickets, all very strange.

She went to give me a lickin' but I ran—I was trying to draw musical notes on staff paper, five years old, I was sitting on the floor using a footstool as a table. In a characteristic fit of rage I kicked the stool, maddened by the failure of my efforts. She chased me to give me a lickin', she turned me over a chair in the living room in the bright white morning, she had me down but my one hand over my bum trying to protect it held a pen.

The pen went clean through her hand with the force of the blow—memory of her standing screaming with stunned disbelief, shock, looking at her palm just starting to bleed, pen protruding from both sides of the hand like a fake protruding arrow through someone's head—the blood then starting to flow thick and ketchup-like down her wrist.

She swore cusswords with the pain, called Aunt Maxine and Uncle Elmer to take her to the hospital—in the waiting room the utter, dour, sour silence of adults, me knowing the first stabs of guilt, blame, shame, self-reproach. What words are there to say to the child who would do such a thing to his own mother? Especially by the normal day-in-day-out dreary blind-to-time humble workers in the mine?

The mark of Cain indelibly branded on me that moment— all pretense of innocence stolen away very early by this grim circumstance of chance. Afterwards her bandaged hand an accusative reminder: *What happened to your hand, Mona?*

"Ask HIM what happened!"

All eyes turning and waiting as I stumbled trying to explain. Of course there was no explaining—we're human beings, we hurt each other, it's a bad show… But still in this my fifth year, in the house by the gravel road, by the creek and the dark greenery of the mysterious woods, I sought in my way an explanation as to how and why this should be.

Was it because of the garter snakes I saw sliding through the grass, whose dry smooth flow disturbed me so (especially after sighting a rain-drenched, cardboard wrapping paper spool lying in the forest which I also took to be a huge monster snake), that I determinedly placed thorny branches in the ditch I thought they emerged from in order to kill them?

Was it because of the raccoon I saw rotting by the side of a corn field, half its body brilliantly alive with an infinitude of glistening maggots?

Was it because of the harsh words and the harsh silences of the exhausted bodies at the end of a long day of work, the fierce pain and fury of the parts of them still unresigned and unreconciled to the shapes life was forcing them into—their tongues and hands blindly flailing out as the waves of anger and boredom and wounded pride pulled them back, back from their visions of glory and swept them into the hungry oblivion of old age and death?

Was it because of the bitter and inconsolable misery I sensed, passionately cursing existence behind the masks of goodwill and earnest well-wishing everywhere—the worm of discontent that wriggles behind each amiable smile, the misery that gives the lie to all decency?

But as the seasons turned, the yellow school buses crackled down the leaf-littered gravel roads, and the snow later swamping the roads in a grandstanding display of prodigiousity (closing schools and businesses for miles around), and on the blackest freezing night of Christmas, when in the streaking blear and blur of impossibly colourful lights, so many expectations are raised and so many are mercilessly disappointed, in the thawing muck of springtime when butterflies land on milkweed stalks and the creeks rise turgid, swelling, musty, embarrassing the shores, when the tractors like armadillos nose the awakening earth and the sun rises high to its vantage point, raining its fire upon the land and the lake all through the hallucinogenic empires of summer—as all the fine and brazen youth, who scorn and ridicule the customs and advice and infirmities of their elders, and who then become the elders themselves, their customs and advice and infirmities being scorned and ridiculed by yet another generation of strong and brazen youth—until all ages become consigned to the graveyard, under whose blanket of earth and grass and moss and stone they lie being gradually forgotten, expunged from the minds of all living as the leaves gather on the ground above them, then the ice and the snow, then the rain and the butterflies, then the hot sun heating their gravestones, then the leaves rushing enthusiastically back to provide their yearly throw blanket, as the bodies melt into dust.

Above and beyond the parade of sufferers marching to their graves and the sour drunkenness vandalizing the sacred miracle of consciousness, still in my mind's eye I see a farm-house on a hill, the silence in the air all around it like the soundless infinities of the universe itself, the earth sprawling from all its corners, and up the back steps coming into the kitchen, with the thermometers and the barometers and the clock ticking on its shelf, is an old portly man who through the eyes of a child might be as old as the earth itself, or God, or Santa Claus who says, *Come in! Come in!* and *Won't you stay for supper?*

His working days through—yet it was he and these gentle, mighty hands that had pulled a living from the earth, pulled a life from the soil, drawn out of it this very house and all of its scattered inhabitants and descendants. And of course to the earth he did return, it outlived him, and far after others will pry life from stone, and far before, of course, the Native trod the soil, before the English and Scots and Irish came to steal and squat, and before that massive glaciers one time sailed these fields majestic as any cruise ship.

But for a while there was simply an old man who sat at the kitchen table reading a newspaper through a magnifying glass, who got up periodically to spit his tobacco into the fire of his old stove, who looked out the window and made note of the very occasional cars that slowly passed by, knowing each one and whom they belonged to, who got up and pulled his chair up to the telephone in the next room to make a call, who was lonely and old, who looked expectantly down the road for company, who had thrown a lifetime of work and sweat into the land, who had known hardship and tragedy and sickness, who had found comfort in tissue paper hymnals and sunlight through painted glass and a fifty-year favoured pew, and who still lay in a darkened bedroom and feared death.

For a while there was just an old farmer the world was passing by at the speed of light, and he rose in his plaid shirt, put down his magnifying glass, opened the door and called out, *Well! Come in, come in!* and *You'll be staying for supper, won't you?*

THE HOLE

ON A BRIGHT SUNDAY SUMMER MORNING A YOUNG BOY plays in a hole at the end of the laneway by a gravel road: the purpose of the hole being to serve as a receptacle for an intended fence post—he can crouch in the hole and hide himself entirely from view, looking at the side of the hole, the brown-grey earth freshly dug, cold, damp, with the severed gnarly roots of weeds and assorted stones embedded in it.

From the house (his home) a distance behind him, he hears the voice of his mother shouting angrily, in slash-ing-white flashes like the edges of breaking glass. The boy stands up and turns to see his father come trudging silently from the house with stoic determination, his pace as matter-of-fact and blank as the expression on his face, a bag of golf clubs slung over his shoulder.

The boy ducks down in the hole as his father comes

walking to him, then slowly raises his head to take a quick peek, noting how his father has magically appeared closer in the interim, grown larger. He ducks back down and counts to three, then looks up from the dank clay and cold, quiet smell of the earth to see his father now looming above him against the sky, squinting down the road.

The boy allows his gaze to travel down his father's pants and focuses on his shoes now so close beside him he can see the texture of their canvas, the metal around the eyelets where the laces come through. He hurriedly ducks down again, making enough movement so that his dad will take note of his presence.

"Hey, partner," comes the deep, quiet voice with a chuckle. "Playin' out here in this hole again, eh?" He takes the golf clubs from his shoulder and sets them down on the gravel. The boy looks up at him, his eyes level with the ground, seeing his father's face and shoulders floating high above the blades of wild grass.

"Be sure you don't get those pants too dirty," his father says, pulling a pack of cigarettes from the breast pocket of his shirt.

The boy pulls at a root sticking from the wall of the hole, looking over and up at his dad from the corner of his eye. "Why's Mom yellin'?" he asks.

"Oh, she's mad," his father begins, pausing to light his cigarette and replacing his lighter in his pants, exhaling a swift stream of smoke. He squints off down the road and resumes. "Oh, she's mad, I suppose, 'cause I'm goin' out golfin' and, you know, she don't like that." He stands with one hand in his pocket, smoking his cigarette, gazing down the road.

"How come?" his son asks, now staring at an ant crawling on a leaf at eye level, hearing the constant hum he always hears on bright summer mornings and smelling the different smell cigarette smoke always has outside.

"Oh well, your mother doesn't understand, or..." He pauses, revising his thought before delivering it emphatically to the end of the road, "...doesn't want to understand, I guess, that a man has got to be able to go out and relax himself every so often after he's been workin' like the devil all week long to keep the bills paid." He frowns and shrugs, offering the proposition: "I mean, it's only reasonable, eh? I mean, what the hell, ol' Dad's gotta be able to go out and play sometimes, too, eh?" he asks, looking down at his son in the hole.

"I guess so," says the boy, watching the tiny legs of the ant.

"Sure," says his father, tilting his head. "Go out, see his buddies, have a good time. I mean, what the hell, eh pal?"

The boy looks up at him, smiling, and nods, to not have him ask the question again, as far in the distance a swelling cloud of dust announces a car coming along the road...

"Maybe," the boy says quietly, "if she gets too mad you can come out here and stay in the hole with me, and we can live out here."

His father turns to the car coming up the road, his arm outstretched and waving at it, then he reaches down for his clubs, swinging them over his shoulder as the car comes up, crackling on the gravel. He looks back at his son for a moment, blankly, as if he's forgotten something. "What?" he says, then smiles with a short, surprised laugh. "Thanks, little buddy, but I don't think there'd be enough room for the both of us in there, do you?"

"Hey, Buzz! Let's go!" the men are calling from the windows of the car. There are two in the front seat and two in the back, all smiling and chuckling.

"Right-o!" he replies, jogging over to throw his clubs in the trunk.

"Get out okay this mornin', Buzz?" a grinning red-faced man asks from the front seat as the boy's father reaches for the handle of the door.

He shares a quick teeth-flashing smile with the man then turns to his son as he climbs into the car, pointing at him. "You be good now," he says sternly with a sudden frown, then bows and shoves himself into the back beside the other men. The car door slams and they drive off, the gravel crackling and the dust billowing behind them as they roar down the road.

The boy stands in the hole, crouching low and counting to three, then popping up again, noting how the car grows smaller, suddenly leaps up the road farther. He ducks down again then slowly eases his head up to peer solemnly over the edge of the hole, noting now how the car has suddenly and magically become no more than a distant billow of dust, now shrinking, now dissipating into the still morning air.

A MAN WHO REALLY COULD SEE

IN THE YEARS IN THE COUNTRY ON THE DAYS WHEN OUR parents were working, my brother and I were left in the care of Daddy Jack and Momma Simpson and their family at their pig farm on the highway.

Daddy Jack sits at the kitchen table in the early predawn hours—the sky through the window purple, almost green. He sits there beneath the yellow light bulb, a butt between his fingers, the ashtray before him overflowing with the broken brown tobacco crumbling from the half a pack he smoked before we rose—his face pulpy and clustered, a reddish brown, his large, hawk, Native nose (he's part Chippewa) and his tiny black eyes rimmed with weary satchel bags bespeaking a tiredness and a sadness beyond his years. A FARMER'S CO-OP calendar is on the wall behind him—the month is April.

Fat Momma Simpson serves oatmeal from off the stove.

Daddy Jack don't want any—Daddy Jack don't eat much, mostly just drinks beer. Sometimes when he gets hungry, say three in the morning, he hauls a big steak out from the freezer in the basement, fries it rare and eats it out of the pan, the blood sloshing 'round in the bottom of it.

Now from his bed comes Daddy Jack's son Jack Junior whom they call Bud—his long black hair ruffled up and sticking out all over, tall and thin, his ribs like ladders. He sits down at the table and lights up a smoke. Momma Simpson is talking about the retarded kids again—she does volunteer work with the retarded kids—wants to bring them around to the farm for a day.

"We don't want no fuckin' retards around here!" scoffs Bud, and goes into a spastic impersonation of their motions that makes me laugh.

"You shut UP!" booms Momma Simpson. "Those kids got just as much right to be here as you do!"

Bud scowls and shakes his head, looking down at the end of his cigarette as he taps it out at the ashtray. Daddy Jack chuckles briefly. One time a local retarded boy came over and sat at the table, smiling and nodding all through dinner—after he left Daddy Jack said, "Well I'll be goddamned if that boy ain't the biggest halfwit I ever saw in my life!" And Momma Simpson had yelled, "For Christ's sake Jack, the boy's RETARDED!"

Now Daddy Jack is talking to Bud about farm matters and such, his low, deep voice remonstrating about the feeding of hogs. The combined smoke of their cigarettes chokes me as I eat the porridge. The floor is covered with newspapers stained with mud and pigshit.

Momma Simpson is sucking porridge from her spoon, her lips pursed with a pained expression. She has dreamed of better things, to be sure, a life of ease and decorum, but feared she was incapable of attaining them. Thus she married Daddy Jack, banishing both doubt and dream.

Now Bud and Jack are heatedly discussing the mending of an axle on the grain wagon. "Now goddamnit Bud I tol' you to take that into town yesserday!"

"Ah, I'll take the fuckin' thing in tomorrow," scoffs Bud, his eyes squinting and his lips curling into a sneer.

"Now where's that lazy sonofabitch Harley?" Daddy Jack inquires, looking about. When he gets angry his eyes narrow into tiny slits and the corners of his mouth turn down, looking like he's about to cry.

"Now Jack you leave that boy ALONE!" says Momma Simpson. "Stop givin' him a hard time!"—Harley being Daddy Jack's younger son, Momma Simpson's darling.

"I'm not givin him a hard time..."

"You ride that boy's ass every day of the week," insists Momma Simpson, her voice muffled low and droning, coming from deep in her throat, all coated round and blanketed with fat like a bell ringing in a sock.

"Shit," Daddy Jack says. "HARLEY!"

Out comes Harley, dreary and bleary, his hair sticking up like dry straw, his mouth agape, his fat bare belly sticking out. Saliva drips from his lower lip. "Goddamn..." he mumbles, all weary

"I was gonna throw a glass a water on ya!" Daddy Jack says.

Harley shakes his head like a horse. "Piss," he murmurs.

Momma Simpson looks at Harley with loving eyes. "You gonna have some porridge?" she asks.

"I was gonna grab ya by the toe an' pull ya flat on your ass outta that bed," Daddy Jack says, chuckling.

Harley slams down in his chair and looks about with glazed uncomprehending eyes.

"You want some porridge?" Momma Simpson asks.

"No goddamn time!" Daddy Jack snaps. "We gotta get those chores done!"

Bud and Daddy Jack pull themselves up from the table. "C'mon Harley!"

"I'll be out in a minute," Harley groans, his face buried in his hands.

"You come out now!" Daddy Jack shouts.

Bud adds, "You got outta doin' chores yesterday!"

"Fuck," moans Harley.

"Jack he just got UP!" Momma Simpson implores.

"Shit!" exclaims Daddy Jack, but he and Bud bend and pull their big black barn boots on by the door, caked with clumps of mud and shit. My brother and I follow them down the steps and out the back door.

"I'll give that kid a tin ear one a' these days," mutters Daddy Jack as he hits the screen door open and it goes vibrating, jangling, springing back and forth on its hinges slamming against the wall and away and we step out to the cold sun rising over the cornfields in the grey, misty sky, the cold dew shining, the cold world sleeping, the cold warmth creeping over every breathing leaf. We walk through the tall grass of the yard past discarded automobile parts, farm equipment, a long unused plough, a big charred oil barrel they use to burn their garbage in. The grass is rustling and twinkling with the dew, the sun shining into the curls and corners of Daddy Jack's leathery face.

"Best goddamned time a' the day," he says, squinting. He throws back his head and horks a big green blob that splatters onto an old, rusty hubcap on the ground, dribbling down and shining in the sun. The earth is frozen and smeared with snot, everything is speckled with dew. Even dreary pieces of lumber and cardboard garbage shine, and the swift breeze bites us all the more for the wiry warmth of the sun behind us. Make no mistake about it, the harsh elements sting the things of this world into awakening.

The clouds tremble in the sky above and we look over to the side and see Lady the Dog hopping her way through the wet grass. My brother and I, we run to greet her—and with a quick move she recoils from our touch and pads disinterestedly away.

"Hey! Don't bother Lady," Daddy Jack shouts. "Lady don't wanna play no more."

"What? How come?" we ask.

"Lady gettin' old. She's an old dog." Lady walks away. Her eyes flash back, blinking, irritated—her grizzled black dog lips in a frazzled frown.

"So?" we ask.

"So! Old dogs don't like to play. Try and she's likely to bite ya. Old dogs just like to be off by themselves. They don't like to piss around."

"Why?"

"'Cause they wanna be alone; they're tired and sick, they're sick of it all." As if hearing us, Lady hobbles over and creeps underneath a truck in the green dewy grass—puts her head down on her paws, her eyebrows twitching. "Yup—ol' dogs, they just like to be off by themself—they get mean, cranky. Ya leave 'em alone—they don't like to chase rabbits and they don't like kids. They just wanna go off, off by themself, then one day... they go off and they don't come back no more and that's it."

"Where do they go?" we ask.

"They go off and die is where they go. They know they're gonna die, so they go off so they can die all alone."

"Why?"

"'Cause that's just the way they wanna do it; they go off because they wanna die all by themself."

"Why?"

"Jesus Christ, how 'n hell do I know? That's just the way they do it!"

"But Lady useta like to play with us," we say.

"That was before when she was young and nice—now she's more 'n likely to bite ya. Don't ask me why, that's just the way it is—old dogs get mean," says Daddy Jack.

We look back at Lady sitting finicky like an old woman, holding her spindly bones together, not understanding how she has been transformed, remembering the old Lady, quick to run and eager to please—lost, but where?

We advance to the barn, Daddy Jack unbolts the door and switches on the lights. There in the dust and the sweet smells of grain and straw and the heavy brown odour of shit so strong it makes you sneeze, wedged into their pens row upon row in the suddenly illuminated precincts the round-backed, swelling bellied, pink, hairy hogs nuzzle and complain.

A cacophony of squeals and wails erupt and arise from the multitude of pigdom, long drawn-out issuances of irritation do they oink and blare, heads down low and scruffling the ground, phalanxes of big fat rumps almost like human asses wobbling from side to side as they stomp their hooves, their curly, whirly, squiggle-tails bobbing, their beady eyes blinking with forbearance, their slobbering and dripping, drooling mouths with little surprising shoots of sharp whiskers here and there about their snouts; they squeak and squeal at the sudden light.

"C'mon Bud!" Daddy Jack barks. "Git the shovels!"

With haste the father and son wearily hoist the shovels from off the pegs on the wall and with resigned resolution they set upon their task, marching down the rows of stalls and scraping from the concrete the moist brown puddings of shit from beneath each squeaking pig's ass. Their faces are set into expressions of grim practicality, their mouths downturned, their noses quivering, their eyes squinting as they look down at the poop they're scraping up. It's a hard smell to get used to—every so often Bud goes *Phew!* and shakes his head with distaste.

My brother and I follow them with wheelbarrows into which every so often the big, slimy cakes of shit are shoved into, sliding off the shovels. At the end of each row we run the wheelbarrows outside and empty them onto the great big mountain of shit behind the barn, then go running back to follow behind Daddy Jack and Bud as they start the next row. Sometimes the pigs get in the way of the shovelling and Daddy Jack has to whack them on the ass with his shovel, crying, "Git on, ye!" and the pig trembling on his little, stubby legs shifts sideways squealing. And sometimes Daddy Jack whacks them for no reason.

"I'd like to know where that lazy sonofabitch Harley is!" Bud shouts out above the thundering grunts and whines and screams and yelps of the hogs as he lifts a particularly heavy brown deposit on the end of his shovel.

"Ah, it's that mother a yers!" gripes Daddy Jack scraping, sweat streaming from beneath his John Deere tractor hat. "She gonna coddle and baby the little cocksucker till he's an old man."

Scrape, scrape, scrape, plopping thick and stickily with a smacking *quirlppkkk* sound off the end of the shovels, wheeled around and loaded off into the big mountain of shit, the ultimate destination of everything, drying and hardening and blackening into an ossified crustiness, a moat of puddles and rivers of liquified shit surrounding it, breeding place of maggots, humming and vibrating with every conceivable type of fly, buzzing black speckles jiggling in the sky, flies in your eyes, on your face, in your food, big fat flies that bite and when you kill them leave red blotches on your arms. Flies swarming the eyes of the pigs, squirrelling into their nostrils, into the flaps of their ears, flies buzzing impatiently around the buttocks of the pigs, flies, flies, flies.

And after many trips to the mountain of shit the last cakey, squishing dollop is consigned with the last plopping smack plastered into the overwhelming tingling stench. We go back and Daddy Jack and Bud sift the grain into the pigs' feeders, the greedy, slopping big mouths of the hogs nuzzling and swilling it down their gorges, their squeals relenting and giving way to low, satisfied grunts and groans as they cram their heads into the steel feeders in pure orgiastic frenzy, gulp, gulp, gulp.

Daddy Jack removes his cap and wipes his wet forehead, watching them expressionlessly. Afterwards, it's breeding time for a choice boar and sow. Father and son lead the hogs out of their stalls and into an aisle between the rows. "Come on, c'mon, there, git on, ye!" shouts Daddy Jack, slapping their rumps. The sow seems eager enough, but the boar hangs back, sniffing the ground, disinterested. "Bring 'im around here!" Daddy Jack orders Bud.

Bud grabs the pig by the head with both hands and tries to get him into position, shoving his snout into the crotch of the sow. The swine shakes his head away and looks dumbly off in the other direction. "I'm tryin', dad!" Bud exclaims. "He jes' ain't interested!"

"Goddamn!" Daddy Jack yells, runs over and grabs the pig's head and shoves it right up to the rump of the other pig. "Now, now, you check, Bud!" Daddy Jack gasps, his face red and sweating with the effort of holding the squirming pig's face in the crotch of the sow.

"Check what 'is cock's doin'. HURRY UP now, god-damnit!"

Bud bends down, squints his eyes, shakes his head. "Nothin', Dad!"

"Well God-DAMN!" cries Daddy Jack, shoving the hog away. "Whatta we got—the bastard's a goddamn faggot or somethin!" He shakes his head and spits angrily. "Well, only one thing we can do," he mutters and begins to remove his gloves.

But just then we hear the barn door slam and turn to see

Harley trudging sulkily up the aisle between the rows. Daddy Jack looks over at Bud and grins. "Hey! Harley! Git yer ass over here!" he shouts as Bud laughs. "We gotta JOB fer ya!"

Harley looks up in surprise for a moment, then scowls. "Ah, fuck, how come I always get stuck with that shit?" he snorts, pouting, kicking his boot against the wall.

"Git yer ass over here!" Daddy Jack shouts and chortles triumphantly with Bud as Harley strides over, angrily pulling off his gloves.

❖

Momma Simpson at the kitchen table stares blinking over her empty bowl with her tongue inside her mouth vacantly swishing milky remnants of porridge. Her large white forearms rest upon the table right at the point where her dimpled elbows swell up into the meaty, milky vastness of her upper arms, the fat seemingly powerful to have once caused my brother to remark admiringly upon her "big muscles." These very arms are speckled with black-red scabs caused by her inability to refrain from scratching her mosquito bites until they bleed.

Now Momma Simpson's eyes narrow into squints as she stares in the quiet kitchen, the only sound being the white clock radio on top of the fridge humming country western music. She is cooking up a crisis—her particular philosophy being that since stumbling blocks are due to always come anyway, why the trick then is not to avoid them but to welcome them, in fact to perhaps create and foster them wherever possible, the idea being that once one has inured and reconciled oneself to the worst then there are really no problems in life (this not thought through in a conscious way in her mind but instinctively sought for at a lower subconscious level in her mechanism).

Thus every molehill mutates inflating into a troublesome mountain beneath her gaze and touch, and she like a bee gathering pollen flits from deathbed to deathbed and ministers to the weary sickly organisms, collecting and distilling their feverish misery, the wicked, white blow of death deep within her gullet—all the better to steel herself for the unspeakable tragedy which is always on its way, inevitable.

Likewise does she, with immaculate solicitude, shower care and compassion upon the mentally defective, the ones born simple, slow, their eyes set wide apart, innocent and uncomprehending, destined all alike to perish young and no further enlightened as to why this should be so—the utter explosive unfairness of this, it is, he is, you are, that's all—all founded and predicated upon a reality which is unacceptable to mere mortal minds.

To Momma Simpson this is the Ultimate Backdrop of Reality before which we play our foolish Punch and Judy show of life: disease and misery are not aberrations but rather well-being and happiness are, mere brief intervals in the ongoing rush of death and decay—and as such, are to be savoured and prized, transient though they may be.

Never does she perceive a rose but that its oncoming blight and withering are immediately perceptible to her— and never even on the brightest day does the sun shine bright enough to erase the hungry black mist encroaching around its circumference—and never does the human form present itself but that she sees the oncoming ashiness of face, the grizzled limbs, the palsied hands, the hard bone of skeleton impatiently awaiting release.

It is for this reason her bleeding mosquito bites and scabs, her jabbering mouth never ceasing to detail the latest catastrophe, crisis, hectoring on into the deep night when the mood takes her, causing poor old Daddy Jack to clasp his head with trembling hands (he is a great sufferer of migraines) and with an almost-weeping expression on his wincing face cry, "Grace. Please, just STOP it. JESUS!"

For stumbling blocks must and will come with admirable efficiency and haste, while miracles are oft lost in the mail. It's always something and if it isn't it soon will be, and so it is in the grim comfort of imminent and utter devastation that Momma Simpson unreservedly and trustfully places the whole of her faith.

Now Momma Simpson rises from the table with her empty bowl, turns and rinses it out in the sink. She stands before the sink and looks out the little window above it, sees the misty cornfields and the Jacksons' barn a half-mile away, sees the desolate highway and the little black sparrows on the drooping hydro lines.

Jack surely does ride that boy's ass, she thinks in her mind— never gives him a moment's peace at all, always on at him about something that means nothing from morning till night. Pickin' on him and pickin' at him, trying to break him down. Well, soon the tale will be told because it was the very same way for Bud when he reached Harley's age, 'round the time of comin' into high school.

For a year there he would not let the boy alone, always gripin' and bitchin' at him about something until finally, suddenly one night he was drunk as a skunk and came on at Bud about his missing hammer, yes the missing hammer, always something stupid like that. Jack came at him drunk and red-faced and screaming, spit comin' out of his mouth, and he pushed Bud back on the couch and Bud's feet came up at Jack and he kicked at him. "Did you see that? Did you see that little cocksucker take a kick at me?" Jack shouted.

"Leave the boy alone!" Momma Simpson said but Jack reached down to grab him by the collar and Bud rose up and hit Jack in the face and Jack staggered back and fell crashing so that the floor and walls of the house all shook and clattered and his head hit the wall and the dishes rattled in the china cabinet. Jack just lay there on the floor for the rest of the night, stinking of the booze. Momma Simpson could tell Bud had not wanted to do it and felt bad, but Jack never did bother him again that way from that time on.

And now Harley's comin' up to that age and Bud and Jack both gang up on him, but it won't be long now. Harley's fillin' out, those arms of his are gettin' bigger, likely he'll grow half a foot in the next year, and if he won't be able to beat Jack sober then he'll surely be able to beat Jack drunk. Momma Simpson lays down the dishrag and clears up the table—feeling a certain pity for her husband, a certain apprehension for the beating he'll take, but knowing there's nothing she can do about it. Might as well try and stop the sun coming up. Oh well, just more proof that this life is a struggle and a heavy yoke to be borne and endured.

❖

There is a stumbling and a clambering at the back door as Daddy Jack, Bud, Harley, my brother and I come in from the barn stamping our big black barn boots at the door, all caked with mud and shit. Daddy Jack's gravelly voice rumbles on about the axle on the grain wagon: "Gotta go to town to get the axle on the grain wagon fixed since Bud didn't git it done yesserday."

"Ah shit, I said I'd take it in tomorrow!" grumbles Bud but Daddy Jack says he wants to git 'er done today, and he'll need Harley and Bud to hoist it in and out of the pickup—the Ole Clunker they call it, an ol' truck from 1957.

"There goes my fuckin' day," moans Harley.

"Stop yer bitchin'," Daddy Jack snaps and grunts as he strains upon a chair changing from his barn boots into his town boots.

"Oh," Momma Simpson says, "I gotta go into town to take a casserole to the Henderson's funeral."

"Well hurry the hell up!" mutters Daddy Jack as he changes his hat. My brother and I are excited because we're all going into TOWN and Momma Simpson pulls the pan from the fridge and Harley and Bud go out to get the axle and we all stamp out to the Ole Clunker.

Daddy Jack leaps in the front and fires up a smoke, Bud and Harley come struggling across the yard with the axle ("Slow the fuck down!" shouts Harley, "Keep yer fuckin' end up!" yells Bud) and Daddy Jack guns the engine which comes clanking, quivering, revving, shaking, grinding, turning over with a chugging sound and then with a blast like the world splitting in half, the Ole Clunker starts pounding and vibrating, voluminous clouds of exhaust in the back.

Daddy Jack reaches under the seat and pulls out a bottle with a mouthful of warm beer left in the bottom which he sucks back with a smacking sound then pitches it out the window. Momma Simpson jogs out with her casserole covered over in cellophane, her whole body flapping and flopping, going on about something about the Henderson's funeral, but Daddy Jack just yells out with a sharp shake of his head, "Git in the truck, woman. Jesus ye give a dog's ass a heartburn!" and guns the truck again as Bud and Harley hoist the axle into the back and then jump in after it.

Momma Simpson crawls in the front with us, and all is a big thrill and a calamity and a commotion because we're all going into town, and though nobody even smiles there is a special thing about going into town but only if you have a reason to do so, and as we do in this particular case then everything is all set, this is a special day, and with a roar the Ole Clunker backs across the grass and vrooms down the driveway, clouds of exhaust and dust and gravel crackling and flying up everywhere.

We swerve out onto the highway, Daddy Jack's tiny eyes watching the road expressionlessly as he taps his cigarette at the window, Momma Simpson going on about the funeral: "Never sick a day in his life till the cancer, started out a bump on his back, dumb doctor didn't know nothin.'" But there'd be a good lunch at the reception.

The hydro lines bob and jiggle at each side, barns, houses, horses, forests, farms and fields, swelling and shrinking, Johnson's Variety, Pepsi-Cola and sky all up above, the yellow-rimmed clouds and the sun going higher, the white line of the highway and in the back Harley and Bud smoke crouched on the floor watching everything disappear.

Harley kneels and shoves his face out into the cold wind, sees Happy Henry the Bible Freak up ahead, hobbling along the highway shoulder in his long black overcoat, his long thin legs slicing as he strides like he's a walking pair of scissors, his tiny head bobbing forth and back as if he's counting each step he takes in his head, both arms rigid and loaded down with heavy suitcases containing pamphlets and bibles.

"Bud!" shouts Harley and Bud looks as they come abreast of Happy Henry and Harley horks out a truly incredibly large membrane of green-grey mucous which slides out as if in slow motion, hovers and flaps in the air for a moment till caught by the wind, then is sent splatting and wrapping itself around the head of Happy Henry, whose suitcases go thudding to the earth as his hands fly to his face and Harley and Bud howl with brotherly delight as Henry's frantic figure goes shrinking into the distance.

And in the front Momma Simpson still goes on about the bump and the cancer and Daddy Jack just sighs from time to time, squinting into the sun's bright glare sending a white fuzz shooting into our eyes despite the visor flap, but you get the idea Daddy Jack doesn't even hear Momma Simpson anymore just by the way he smokes his cigarette, and in a minute he starts talking in the middle of one of her sentences in a quiet, thinking kind of way.

"Ya see that bird on that sign up there?"—the sign says TRAILERS FOR RENT—"Well my dad coulda not only seen that bird, he coulda tol' ye what kind of a bird it was, not only from the distance we just were, but from a good half-mile back more 'n that," he mutters.

And now Momma Simpson is silent, like he isn't interrupting what she was saying, like she can't even remember
talking in the first place. She watches the bird as Daddy Jack
blows out a big cloud of cigarette smoke and stubs his cigarette in the ashtray.

"When he was seventy-nine he could see things even more
farther away than I ever could, way out to hell and back. 'Jack,'
he'd say, 'can you see the colour a that pickup goin' down the
fifth line?' Well, I'll be goddamned if I could..." Daddy Jack
says, more like he's talking to himself, or to somebody else
who isn't even here. "Seventy-nine, never wore glasses a day
in his life. Now that was a man who really could see."

HAPPY HENRY

AND WHAT OF HAPPY HENRY, SPINDLY FINGERS NOW blindly clawing Harley's mucous off his face by the highway on this cool April morning? He murmurs and simpers little *mmf* sounds to himself and now a wrinkled tissue is drawn from his overcoat pocket to dispatch the mess. He shakes his head in puzzlement and bends for the suitcases, his Salvation Army shoes encased in plastic bread bags for protection skiffling in the gravel as he resumes his pilgrimage, this rabbit-faced disciple of the Lord, his little grey teeth overhanging his thin lower lip.

He trudges and his undersized head glistening with grease slicking back his short black hair—as if his whole head's been dipped in a vat of oil—resumes its loping pendulum swing. His beady eyes aglow, he stumbles down the lonely morning highway, cars and transport trucks roaring past and whipping him around in their wake and slipstreams of exhaust and dust and ricocheting stones. The tails of his overcoat ruffle, ol' Happy Henry known for miles around, you might see him on the highway, you might see him crossing a distant field, sailing through a sea of weeds, or ambling down a quiet side street in the town, in the night, his shadow passing beneath the beam of a streetlight, darkness and silence all around.

He may accost you in the drugstore or in the barbershop, his shy hesitant smiling face, his stuttering lisping voice asking, "Hello? How are you today?"—for everything he says is said like a question. He blinks and before you know it a pamphlet is being passed into your hand.

ETERNITY IS FOREVER—a picture of the sky: fluffy, white clouds and behind one of them a little piece of the sun peeking around—long lines stretching out from it, reaching to the edge of the paper. HAVE YOU MADE YOUR CHOICE? Inside, WHERE WILL YOU SPEND ETERNITY? IN HEAVEN OR IN HELL?

"Some reading material—for free," says Happy Henry, smiling and bowing slightly, nodding his head towards the pamphlet as you stand there, and as you stuff it into your pocket and thank him, planning to discreetly dispose of it later.

As you turn and depart from him, he stands still behind you, nodding his head and regarding you with glowing eyes— joyful, envying the happiness you will know when you later privately read the pamphlet and its true meaning washes over you, when the glory of the Lord's love rains down over your heart and the truth of your redemption paid for with the price of God's only begotten son detonates across your consciousness and you are truly cleansed in the blood of the lamb.

Yes, Henry knows and anticipates the bounteous future awakening, which will take place, and most of all your incredible surprise at discovering that you are the personal receiver of the greatest gift that has ever been given—Henry's benevolent head nodding, ushering you into that most beautiful and incomprehensible sanctuary, the universe a compassionate womb in love with you forever—*If only you don't drink or smoke or use curse words*, Henry thinks with a stern frown, his brow furrowing.

He strides down the highway up to Barker's Corner, to the gas station with the all-night coffee shop attached, loping up across the parking lot with an energetic spring quickening in his long bony legs. In the front window of the coffee shop three men sit huddled around a table, their coffee cups half-filled before them, their elbows resting on the table and their large boots on the floor resting in gloppy puddles of mud. They wear thick, grey, mud-spattered jackets and hats emblazoned with the logos of various tractor and farm implement manufacturers.

One of the men sits sucking on a pipe that periodically goes out, necessitating that he continually relight it—the ashtray before him filled with blackened matches. The man sitting across from him looks out the window and sees Henry limping his way across the lot.

"Well here comes ol' Henry," he chuckles, his eyes darting across to the other two men.

"That's right. There he is, Roy," drawls the pipe-smoker, "on his way to make another new convert, I suspect."

"Heh, heh," chuckles Roy. "Don't suspect there's any likelihood on 'im makin' a fresh one outta you, eh Gus?"

"Oh, Henry knows me all right," says the other fellow laconically. "I 'magine by this time he knows he'd be barkin' up the wrong tree tryin' to get somewhere with me."

Roy laughs, and the other fellow, an older man with weary, watery eyes chuckles as well as Henry throws open the door of the coffee shop and stumbles in, having a bit of trouble with his sizable suitcases. The middle-aged woman behind the cash register looks up with a bemused smile and the men sitting at the table all turn to him, nod, "How y'doin', Henry?" winking at each other, then return to their conversation.

A newspaper lies on the table in the midst of them, *The Wigford Gazette*, with its tale on the front page of how a discarded refrigerator had been found in a ditch by a sideroad twenty miles out of town the night before, and in the refrigerator was discovered a partially decomposed human body.

"Jesus Christ!" cries Roy. "How d'ya like that? Jesus, somethin' like that ain't happened round here since… well Christ, since ol' Ferguson on the first line did 'is wife in. I 'member that from when I was a kid—musta been forty years ago."

"Yeah, yep, that's right, Roy, I 'member that, sure. Ol' Ferguson he'd been married, what, twenty years to the same woman, came home one night and put an axe right through her head," nods the fellow with wet, weary eyes, his voice soft and untroubled. "Didn't seem to be no rhyme nor reason to it, never a hint there was anything wrong. Just got off work at the gravel pit, came home and put an ax right through 'er head."

"Jesus, yeah!" says Roy, "and I remember my old man sayin' he never could understand it, ol' Ferguson. Christ the guy was one of the funniest devils around, always had a kind word and a prank, never even hardly saw him when he wasn't smilin' or laughin', and one of the main guys at the Presbyterian Church there in town, always at the picnics and such, playin' with the kids, arrangin' the games, y' know, the egg and spoon races."

"Yep," says the other fellow. "Just got off work one night, got in the car, drove home, and put an axe right through his wife's head."

"Christ!" cries Roy, shaking his head.

"Well, they put HIM away for life," says the man dispassionately. "Likely he's still in there if he ain't dead by now. When they came he was still standin' there, holdin' the axe— he jes' went away with them quietly. Yep, they didn't waste no time puttin' him away."

"Good goddamn thing, too," says Roy. "Jesus, imagine somethin' like that…"

"Well, seems to me you guys are fergettin' the case of the Dobbins out Starkway way," says Frank suddenly, leaning into the conversation.

"The Dobbins? Hey, that rings a bell somewhere—the Dobbins…" Roy muses.

"Yeah, well that was likely before yous guys's time," says Frank. "Mighta been forty-five years ago now, they had the farm the Trombleys are at now."

"Oh, yeah."

"Yeah, well young Lou Dobbins out there, he's the guy that blew the heads off his grandparents."

"Jesus Christ, yeah! I do recall hearin' tell of somethin' like that, Frank, yeah!" Roy exclaims, snapping his fingers.

"That's right, that's right," agrees Frank. "Yeah, well, it was like this: this Lou Dobbins guy, both his parents were gone.

Didn't know what happened to 'em—mighta been dead, killed in a car accident or just took off, I don't know, I couldn't tell ya. So he'd been mostly raised by his grandparents on his father's side. In fact, you 'member that old scrap-metal yard out on Highway Six?"

"Oh yeah."

"Yep," says Gus.

"Well they useta own that. Anyways, this young Lou Dobbins fella, he grew up and the old folks looked after 'im and he was a queer bird, worked in the garage in town from the time he was fifteen, you never seen him or heard a peep out of 'im otherwise, and he lived out on the farm with the old folks up till he was about thirty years old. Never broke away, if ya know what I mean, kinda strange—seemed timid, wouldn't say boo to a ghost, and you never saw 'im in town at the dances or what have you at all, or with anybody. So no one never thought nothin' of it, people just generally felt that was his way, I guess.

"So he was still livin' with the old folks when he was thirty years old and then of course naturally by that time he couldn't move out 'cause the old folks by this time were OLD, I mean they couldn't've looked after themselves at all—so young Lou was kinda tied to them if ya know what I mean. They'd looked after him so now I guess he was kinda duty-bound and obligated to look after them.

"'Parently for the last couple a years the old folks were so goddamned old and sick they couldn't even get outta bed— they'd just lay there day and night in their pyjamas, and I guess he had to feed 'em and change 'em and turn them over and I don't know what all. People said they were so old and had laid there for so long that the two of 'em even came to look like each other, couldn't tell 'em apart almost—jes' these two wrinkled-up white shrunk-up little things layin' in bed there, never sayin' a word.

"So one day Lou comes in," says Frank, throwing up his hands, "pulls out a twenty-two-gauge shotgun, and blows their heads off."

"Je—sus CHRIST!" cries Roy, wincing. Gus sits looking at Frank out of the corner of his eye, puffing at his pipe, his head cocked.

"Yep, well you know the power of them twenty-two-gauge shotguns," says Frank.

"Jesus, yes," says Roy. "I got one I take up north for the deers—the POWER of them things."

"Yeah, well you can imagine at point-blank range—blew their heads clean off—and then, the weirdest thing, the guy didn't just stop there. 'Parently he reloaded and cocked the thing again and again—and you know how long it takes to reload one a them things—blastin' away at 'em over and over, I mean, after he must've known they MUST've been dead already. I mean, I say he blew their heads off but there weren't hardly enough to bury, really."

"Good Christ!" cries Roy. "You wonder what in hell would possess a man."

"Well, after that he went down into the cellar where he knew they had a bunch of cash stashed in an old fruit jar, I mean somethin' like twenty thousand dollars," says Frank.

"Ah, so that's it," muses Roy, nodding his head grimly.

"Sure. Lou goes down, takes out the loot and nobody sees him no more. Police had a devil of a time trackin' him down—till finally musta been a week later, up in Birkston, they hear the guy's a regular at some tavern and he's the life of the party, dressed in a brand new, sharp suit with a brand spankin' new car outside stayin' at some fancy hotel up there. Been up there all week I guess, buyin' everybody drinks and bein' everybody's pal. I mean, after all a those years walkin' 'round here like a ghost, ya wouldn't hardly believe it.

"Well, they surrounded the place, tryin' to get him to give himself up peaceful-like. Everybody else came runnin' outta that place as if all the devils in hell was chasin' 'em. All the Birkston cops was standin' outside armed to the teeth—I mean, for all they knew he was armed and dangerous."

"Sure, sure," says Roy, blinking with deep interest, his mouth slightly open.

"Yep," agrees the other man. "So like I say, he's in the bar all alone, everybody, even the waiters and what all hauled their asses outta there pronto—if he was everybody's best buddy just a few minutes ago, he sure as hell wasn't now. And the place is surrounded by cops with their guns out and aimed at the doors and they're callin' out askin' him to come out and surrender peacefully when all of a sudden he comes runnin' outta there crazy.

"He ain't armed, no gun, he jes' comes runnin' out as if he actually believes he's got a chance to get past all those cops standin' in a circle round the entire building. Well of course they don't know he wasn't armed, what the hell, so they shot 'im. Funny thing though, after they shoot 'im he falls down, and while he's dyin' his legs are still movin' around on the ground like he's still runnin'.'"

"Hmph," says Roy.

For a moment the three men sit in silence, considering the table.

"Jesus! Hell of a thing!" remarks Roy with a sigh, shaking his head.

"Well, you can bet one thing," says Gus, stabbing his finger at the newspaper. "When they catch THIS guy it ain't gonna be no pretty sight either."

"Damn right," says Roy. "Some no-good lowdown sonofabitch that'd do somethin' like that."

"Well I was talkin' to Hank down at the station, and he says they don't have much of a lead yet," says Frank. "Best they can say now is they think it musta been someone outta the area—least they're hopin' that—who just came round here to stash the body."

"Jesus, let's hope so. Some rotten bastard like that who'd cut up someone's body like that—hangin' ain't fit for 'im," remonstrates Roy.

"I don't suspect it would be," drawls Gus. "Not unless ye hung him up by one ball and waited for the rest of 'im to come fallin' down."

"Huh! Some asshole like that oughta be shot with a ball of his own shit!" says Roy scornfully, baring his teeth in anger.

"Well, what I'd do with some no-good sonofabitch like that…" volunteers Gus, taking time to relight his pipe afresh and drawing on it, "…is take 'im out into the bush behind my property, sit 'im down on a log, nail 'is balls to it, then push 'im over backwards and leave 'im there."

"Fuckin' right, fuckin' right, Gus!" Roy exclaims as Frank, with his watery, weary eyes, nods his agreement.

✿

Happy Henry at this time has settled himself on a stool at the counter with a cup of tea. From the pocket of his overcoat he has taken a bible and laid it before him on the counter, resting his hands on either side of it, and his head at the end of his long thin neck dances back and forth towards and away from the bible as he studies it, every so often pausing in his concentration to gaze hurriedly about the coffee shop then returning again to the bible, the fingers of his hands clenching and unclenching, the upper area of his body swaying from side to side on the stool.

At this point a massive transport truck pulls off the highway and comes to a slow lumbering *whissshhing* steaming stop in the parking lot outside the window—the cab opens and a compact little man clambers out, the bottom of his boots slapping the pavement as he slams the door and trudges up to the coffee shop, his arms at each side held at a considerable distance from his torso with elbows bent as he walks briskly in through the door, an angry frown fixed on his granite face as he steps up to the counter.

"Coffee! Regular!" he commands, and stands shaking his leg impatiently as he waits for it. He's wearing grease-stained blue jeans and a T-shirt with a jacket over it, the zipper half down. He strides with his coffee past the group of men who glance up at him as he passes. He rewards them with an angry glare and drops with a thud into a nearby chair, his hands clasped around the coffee cup, staring stoically before him with a sort of abstract, floating, all-encompassing hostility— the lower half of his face covered with a rash of black prickly whiskers. He perspires heavily from beneath the cap clamped tightly down on his head, the visor of it shadowing his eyes and the bridge of his nose.

Happy Henry swivels on his stool and looks shyly over at the man. Feeling his gaze, the man turns to Henry and stares balefully at him, like a bear through the bars of a cage. His eyes widen as Henry smiles, lifts himself from the stool and comes hobbling over to his table. The man's mouth falls half-open in outraged surprise as he looks up at Henry and Henry says, "Some reading material? For free…" while placing a pamphlet gently on the table before the man, bowing slightly and smiling.

The man's eyes slowly tear themselves from Henry and take in the pamphlet—ETERNITY IS FOREVER. He stares sullenly down at the words—HAVE YOU MADE YOUR CHOICE?—and then cranes his head slowly up to Henry again. His mouth hardens into a compressed, furious sneer and his dark eyes beam at Henry, smouldering with hatred.

Henry smiles and nods, licking his lips. "You've accepted Lord Jesus as your own personal saviour?" he asks pleasantly.

The man parts his lips slightly, revealing the tiny tightly clenched white teeth. His eyebrows arch and his eyes widen and his glistening, sweating face shudders with rage—the coffee in his cup quivering and splashing up over the side.

Henry looks down at the man and a faint doubt causes his smile to falter. "You… you've been cleansed in the blood of the…" he begins, but the man leans forward and a deep guttural sound, something like a growl, burbles up from his throat behind his clenched teeth, causing Happy Henry to step away hurriedly, blank faced, feeling the tiny hairs on the back of his neck prickle up in a quick, cool wave as he shuffles back from the man, something in the man's dark eyes causing his heart to skip a beat as his hands jerk in little aftershocks.

Happy Henry stands in the centre of the coffee shop floor, his eyes troubled and unfocused, until he turns and spies at a table in the far corner, a gentleman sitting peacefully paging through a newspaper, a middle-aged man of average height in a sky-blue shirt neatly tucked into his pants, wearing a brown corduroy sport coat, his calm eyes perusing the paper from behind silver-framed spectacles, his placid mouth a thin gentle curve within the strands of his trim, conservative beard. Henry approaches the man meekly, shyly observing his absorbed and down-tilted profile as he reads the paper; he makes ready with a pamphlet.

"Good morning…" Henry lisps timidly.

The man's head lifts from the paper, his distracted eyes focusing in upon Henry quickly. He smiles pleasantly. "Well, hello, good morning," he says softly, his smile widening, causing friendly wrinkles to form around the edges of his eyes, the irises green and glittering with unguarded warmth from behind his spectacles.

Henry, uncertain, falters a moment in the sincerity of his attention. "H-how are you?" he asks, fingering the pamphlet restively.

"Quite well," replies the man generously, nodding. "And you?"

"I'm… very fine!" exclaims Henry, his head suddenly pumping up and down on the end of his long skinny neck like a piston.

The man stares at Henry, smiling, blinking with bemused

forbearance. His eyes take in the sight of the strange, trembling, black-coated individual before him with a sort of cheerful, genial curiosity. He folds the newspaper and places it on the table. "Would you like to sit down?" he asks quietly.

Henry nods and seats himself quickly on the edge of the chair, licking his lips and beaming at the man excitedly and all of a sudden it comes out of him in a tumbling, exuberant rush, the pamphlet sliding swiftly across the table: "Some reading material," he offers, his upraised eyes glistening hopefully.

"Mm-hm," the man says, glancing cursorily down at the pamphlet. He looks up at Henry and with a sigh he reclines back in his chair. "My name's Sam," he says, extending his hand across the table.

"Henry," says Henry, grasping the man's hand hungrily and shaking it. "Have you accepted the Lord Jesus as your personal saviour?"

The man smiles wistfully, glancing down at the pamphlet. "Well," he says.

"The Lord Jesus loves you," murmurs Henry, "and He wants you to know that whatever sins and bad things you've done are forgiven... an'... and've been paid for up on the cross... for as God's only begotten son, He has died so that we may... may live and know His love and mercy of God's grace." He whispers breathlessly, his body bending towards the man, his neck craning and the features of his pale face gyrating with a terrible urgency.

"Mm-hm," says the man.

"An'... an' to be lifted up into heaven to sit upon the right side of the Lord. Not to fall into the eternal fire and weeping and gnashing of teeth of... of..."

"Hell," says the man.

"An'... an' to trust in the mysterious ways of the Lord, for the wages of sin is death," recites Henry, his eyes closing as if his speech is written on their inner lids. He sways a bit in the chair.

"Mm-hm, well, yes," says the man, nodding thoughtfully. He considers Henry for a moment, smiling faintly, his eyes peering hospitably through his glasses yet at the same time detached, removed, as if observing the situation from an incalculable distance through a telescope. "You attend a church in the area, do you?" he asks.

"Oh, yes. Yes... I attend many churches," replies Henry enthusiastically. "I go to the Harveston Presbyterian, the St. Luke Lutheran, the Baysfield United, the St. Paul Anglican, the Mandaumin United, the Lawford Pentecostal, the..."

"Mm-hm, yes, I see," says the man.

"...the Wigford Baptist, the Point George Anglican, the Wigford Presbyterian..."

"Mm-hm," says the man, looking down for a moment. "Actually," he notes, checking his wristwatch, "I'm heading into Wigford myself. Perhaps I could give you a lift if you're heading in that direction."

"Oh—yes, yes, I'd be very grateful for that, sir," Henry enthuses. "If you'll just... Yes..." he murmurs, jumping up from his chair and moving to the counter where he left his suitcases, gathering them up hurriedly.

The man smiles and chuckles inwardly at Henry's frenetic bustling as he rises leisurely with his rolled-up newspaper and walks towards the door, Henry following at his heels, stumbling with the cases and whispering fervently to himself as he shuffles past Roy and Gus and Frank at their table.

"Well—looks like ol' Henry's got himself a new convert," observes Frank archly.

"Yep, yep, sure does, Frank," says the other man, tamping down his pipe.

"Heh, heh," laughs Roy, shaking his head. "Shee—it!"

And the sun like a gleaming, white, shining nickel now one quarter of the way creeping up the sky through the torn, ragged clouds, beams down upon the man named Sam rustling his keys from his pocket and Happy Henry tramping behind him as they make their way across the parking lot to the car. Sam assists Henry with his cases, packing them away in the back seat.

Now pulling out of the lot onto the highway, Sam a man who enjoys driving, the wheel firm beneath his gently guiding hands as he's leaned back far in his bucket seat, his profile serene, his eyes placidly and without resistance drinking in the road which runs straining and feeds itself disappearing beneath the hood of his car. Happy Henry at his side staring straight ahead, off and up to where the road wedges to its fine point on the horizon, the clouds shifting slowly overhead, the fence posts rushing swiftly forth and multiplying themselves endlessly.

Henry sees them and beyond them and in a most profound manner, sees them not at all, blanketed and overthrown as they are by the thick veil hanging always before his eyes: the veil ruffling and shimmering and composed of all his most fervent convictions and apprehensions, his highest-hoping anticipations and the passion of his highly excitable knowing, which in fact compose and funnel the perceptions of these eyes and is thus more real than all that stands or passes before them— real because true and knowingly grasped as such, the world at large fluidly streaming around to either side and washing over them yet never gaining foothold—merely rippling, trickling, subsiding, dripping, transparent, tasteless, fading, evaporating, waning, gone. Nothing is real but what is true.

Nothing is true except what is necessary, nothing is necessary except that each human soul must be saved from its own sins (whose wages are death) by the love of Jesus Christ, to know that love and trust it and live it and feel it gathering and solid in the entrails, hard, coiled, firm, in the chest and lungs, stretching out along the furthermost limits of the limbs, and deep within the narrow confines and crevices of the brain.

And so Henry turns to Sam, blinking meekly. "Jesus loves you," he whispers tentatively, almost like a question, bending over from his seat, his eyes searching and hopeful.

"Mm-hm," says Sam, guiding his car from the highway onto the road into Wigford, shifting gears. He turns and smiles at Henry. "Beautiful day, isn't it?"

He turns back to the road. "Do you live around these parts? I'm from out of town myself, just here on a little business," Sam muses reflectively, the sun gleaming on the rims of his spectacles and on his beard.

"A lot of nice country around here," Sam remarks after a moment, his eyes taking in the broad flowing fields passing by the window, the fences and the little farms sailing past. "Quite a difference from the big city," he smiles, turning to Henry, his expression warm and inviting, his words flowing out easily with a breezy goodwill.

"I... I live with Father," Henry volunteers, looking straight ahead, his eyes darting sideways to the stranger.

"Hm," says Sam. "And he's a big one for attending church too, I suppose, is he?"

"Oh, no, no," Henry replies. "He cannot walk. He stays inside of the house. He... he takes care of the house... he... but he reads the Bible," Henry pronounces, nodding his head assertively.

"Mm-hm. Handicapped, is he?" Sam notes. "And your mother, she's not around?"

"Oh no, no," says Henry emphatically, shaking his head from side to side, closing his eyes. "She... went away after... She was sick for a long time and she went away... an'... then we buried her away in the ground... because she was sick and then she went away..." he stutters quickly, his voice like a recording played at double speed, high and nasal.

"Hm," says the stranger. "Died, did she?"

"But... but... she was a sinner," murmurs Henry, his eyes glazing over as his mouth moves awkwardly, straining, little drops of spit jumping from the furiously working lips. "She said no to the Lord Jesus, and she used many curse words, even though she was sick for a long time in the bed. She... closed her heart against Jesus and cursed Him and cursed Father and Father was very angry, an'... said she was damned to go to hell... an'... even though Father told her many times, she cursed Jesus and cursed Father, an'... even when her legs turned black... an'... she was very sick..."

"Mm-hm," says the stranger, nodding slightly, his features

taking on a serious cast, his eyebrows narrowing as if deeply involved in the problem being discussed.

"An'... an'... me and Father prayed for her even though Father told me and told her she was damned to go to hell and she shouted curse words back at him still. Father said we should pray for her soul, but not after she went away... for Father said we shouldn't pray for her then, not then when she was gone," Henry says hurriedly.

❁

As Henry says this, the veil in his mind splits and parts like a curtain and opens onto the scene of an aged man sitting in a wooden kitchen chair, naked, a dusty blanket over his lap and resting upon the blanket an open bible. He sits before an old-fashioned wood stove glowing red with the crackling fire within it, his deep-set furious eyes staring at the stove, gold and yellow shards of reflected light from the flames dancing over his clenched, wizened features, his creased forehead, his hollow cheeks, his grimly compressed mouth.

The old man's long, white, snowy hair sweeps from his temples and tumbles back from behind his ears onto his thin bony shoulders and his wrinkled, sinewy hands grasp at the arms of the wooden chair with such force that the veins along the backs of them stand up in thin, bluish ridges and his chest heaves as he breathes long, quavering, determined draughts of air in and out through his nostrils, his chest red and weathered beneath coils of wiry white hairs.

He stares into the fire of the stove angrily, his jaw working back and forth with an outraged, livid fury not entirely of this world. A wooden cross is nailed to the wall above the stove and on the wall behind him his saviour stares skyward with large, long-suffering, soulful eyes from an oval-shaped framed print, His right hand uplifted in a gesture of peace and also of supplication. Pieces of broken glass lie on the floor at the old man's feet, and at the side of his chair is an overturned dish caked with the congealed remains of a long ago, half-eaten dinner.

The old man sits and stares, and around and above and piercing through the rumble of his sonorous breathing are ravening, cascading sheets of sound, the brash, pure, high, metallic shattering sounds of a woman's screams, breaking over his head and ears, the white, blasting, frozen, howling, consciousness-shredding sounds of hysteria and gut-wrenching, horror-filled pain, the broken anguished words rawly torn from the lungs and bloodily hurling the vilest and most graphically wounding curses invented since the dawn of the spoken word, the ringing gale of vengeance and hatred and disgust wrenched from the marrow of the bone and sent screaming in delirious, scalding waves of white noise crashing through the room, the voice breaking and splintering into rough, moaning gasps from time to time as if in disbelief at the extremity of its own suffering.

The old man sits like a stone carving in the midst of it, his large, clear, pain-filled eyes unblinking. His thin, parched lips can be seen to be moving slightly, mechanically, as if repeating a vow or an oath or a ritualistic chant. "The mother of harlots and the abominations of the earth ..." his low rumbling voice repeats, trembling with emotion, "... drunken with the blood of the saints, and the martyrs of Jesus."

✲

"And then Father said that it was well that she died," Henry says. "For she had so offended the Lord that surely misfortune and enmity would be visited upon her the rest of her days, for she was BAD," Henry says, nodding solemnly to himself. "She… was a BAD woman."

"Mm-hm," Sam says, gazing out the window abstractedly.

"An'… an' so we buried her in the ground and Father took her picture down," Happy Henry concludes.

"Hm," says Sam. "We're coming up to the area where the church is right now, aren't we?" he asks, looking around as the car rolls into Wigford, past the IGA grocery and the line of grain wagons pulling up to the granary by the feed store across from Bickerman's Lumberyard by the railroad crossing and the train tracks bisecting the town. People are striding in and out of the grocery, going into Andy's Restaurant for lunch, paying their bills at the bank (checking pieces of paper and passbooks as they emerge and clamber into their pickups)—the bustling activity of the people revving up as the morning flowers open and progresses.

"Um… oh yes," says Henry, extricating himself from his trance and seeing for the first time his surroundings, craning his neck and looking about. "Right down that street there," he says, pointing.

"Mm-hm," says Sam as he pulls the car over to the side of the road. "That would be the Wigford Baptist, would it?"

"Oh yes, they have a fine minister there, Reverend Palmer, a very fine minister," Henry lisps excitedly, his eyes regaining their sparkle.

"He is, is he?" notes Sam, his quietly amused, heavy-lidded eyes considering Henry warmly.

"Oh yes, sometimes the cleaning people are angry… an'…
an' don't like to let me into the church, and I say to them Reverend Palmer says I can come in, and they say 'No, the church
is closed till Sunday,' and that I should go home, but then…
then… I tell Reverend Palmer and he goes and TELLS them.
He says Henry is allowed in anytime. He tells them… that
they are WRONG," says Henry, frowning with severity, his
eyes flashing sternly. "He goes and he says to them that they
are WRONG and he says that Henry can come in ANYtime,
anytime he wants, he says!" Happy Henry nods his head
grimly to punctuate the tale.

"He does, does he?" asks Sam, smiling.

"Yes… He says that the church is God's house and not
the cleaning people's and he says Henry is allowed in ALL
the time, an' he tells them that they are WRONG!" Henry
repeats, his voice rising with his recollected anger.

"Well… that seems a nice thing for him to do, eh?"

"An'… an' so the cleaning people know, because Reverend
Palmer told them all," Henry says.

"Mm-hm," says Sam, looking off and around the town.

"An'… but some ministers do not do this, they say I must
go," Henry continues. "But then some other ones say I may
stay." He smiles, reaching down for his big leather-bound
bible and bringing it up on his lap.

"They do, do they?" Sam remarks, looking down with a
trace of trepidation at the bible.

"Oh yes," says Henry, grinning, opening the bible and
taking out a stack of snapshots. He hands one of the pictures

proudly to Sam: a church organ, mahogany brown, against a wall beneath a stained-glass window.

"Mm-hm," says Sam. "Very nice."

"That's… that's one of my favourites… at the Harveston Presbyterian," notes Henry. "And this one from the Longford Pentecostal. And this one," he says, delivering the snapshots to Sam, fingering through them: a succession of organs, some large, their pipes stretching up the walls to the steeples of the churches, others squat and unimposing. One of the pictures shows Henry seated at an organ, his fingers poised above the keyboard, grinning proudly back over his shoulder into the camera.

"Mm-hm, yes. Very nice," notes Sam noncommittally.

"And I go in and they know me and I go in and they let me play!" Henry murmurs excitedly, leaning over and gazing down fondly at the pictures in Sam's hand.

"Mm-hm," says Sam, handing the pictures back to him, looking off through the window, his face expressionless.

"You're off on your way to the church right now, aren't you?" he asks.

"Oh… oh yes!" Henry exclaims, looking about suddenly and shoving his pictures back into his Bible, opening the door of the car.

"I'll help you with your cases," Sam offers, getting out and retrieving Henry's suitcases from the back seat.

"Oh yes, sir. Thank you, sir," Henry says, picking up the cases.

"No problem at all," Sam says, smiling.

"An'… an' if you'd like, sir, I… I'd like to pray for you, sir," Henry whispers suddenly, his face taking on a serious cast.

"You seem like a very fine man, too, so if you'd like, I'd like to witness to you, and offer up a prayer."

"Hm," says Sam. "Well..."

But all of a sudden Henry's hand leaps forth and quickly clasps Sam's hand. Henry's hand is thin and bony, cold with a thin film of tepid moisture, like ripe cheese, the fingers twining around Sam's hand solicitously then freezing into a possessive hold as his head bows and his eyes close, the eyeballs squirming beneath the trembling eyelids. He sighs heavily then takes in a brisk, sweeping breath of air.

Sam gazes down at Henry's fervent head with strained patience, staring down through his heavy-lidded eyes with a stern alertness, his mouth small and unsmiling.

"Lord... Lord... please bless this fine man," whispers Henry in a strange attenuated, beseeching voice, his head now upraised and slowly dancing from side to side like a blind man's. "An'... an'... let his heart be opened to your ways and become cleansed and washed and purified in the blood of the lamb, an'..." His grip relaxes then tightens on Sam's hand. "An' be cleansed in the blood of the lamb—an' be saved from the hellfire of weeping and gnashing... in... the..."

And all around the two men standing by the car, trucks rumble down the main street of Wigford, people pass by on their way to the Variety, a yellow school bus drives through, the windows crowded with clusters of children.

"In the name of the Holy Spirit... and the gnashing and the weeping... an'... this fine, fine man, Lord," Henry mumbles, searching for the familiar words. "An', an'... the blood of the lamb. Amen." His eyes open wide and resume blinking, his shoulders flinch as his soul comes jerking back into his body. "Th-thank you, sir," he stutters to the stranger.

"No problem," replies Sam.

"An'... an' may you have a fine trip, and a nice day..." says Henry, smiling, pressing his hand.

"Fine, fine, no problem," says Sam, extricating his hand briskly and moving to the door of his car.

"An' thank you for the ride, sir!" Henry calls as Sam gets into his car and starts the engine.

Sam smiles back over his shoulder at Henry. "That's fine, no problem. Bye now," he says as he slams the car door and begins to pull away.

Happy Henry stands beaming proudly at the car for a moment as it whooshes from the curb and goes off down Main Street up over the hump of the railroad tracks and sails away. Then he hurriedly collects his cases and limps on to the church.

Sam in his car drives steadily, his placid face trained upon the road. After a moment he reaches down to turn on the radio, paying no particular attention to the music, just hearing the sound. It washes over his consciousness much like the landscape streaming and draining away at the periphery of his vision. His soft eyes blink peacefully behind his spectacles.

COME ALL YE YOUNG LOVERS (I)

BUZZ AND MONA DRIVE THROUGH THE COUNTRYSIDE dusk to the home of George and Martha, George being the brother of Mona. Mona sits behind the wheel as Buzz dislikes driving as a matter of principle: that is, he dislikes driving generally and it's mutually understood between his wife and himself that on any journey they take together, she shall undertake the navigation of the transporting vehicle, particularly on a journey such as this one, towards a function held at the home of one of Mona's family (the occasion being George and Martha's twenty-fifth wedding anniversary), at which Buzz's appearance is always made under a certain amount of duress, a duress given voice to through frequent, heavy sighs and the rebellious token of a bottle of beer taken into the car to be consumed along the way.

The two kids in the back seat are by turns silent and noisome, from time to time erupting in small tussles to which Buzz responds as they reach the threshold of calamity with, "All right, all right now," the peremptory tone of his voice like the bark of a tired watchdog barking more out of habit and duty than anything else, alerting them of the barrier they've transgressed and effectively snuffing their disquiet until the next time, a few minutes later.

The boys sit squirming on the vinyl seat covers, their feet dangling a bit above the car floor as one of them asks Buzz to sing the song about Santa Claus. The other says no, he wants to hear the song about the country boy. The first kid says he asked first, and as they start arguing again, their voices pitched progressively higher, the low rumbling voice of Buzz begins taking flight from the front seat, quietening them as his croon comes up in its glancing devil-may-care manner. His eyes before him on the road, his head cocks to the side as he gestures with an open palm, singing:

> *Just because you think you're so smart*
> *and breaking everybody's heart*
> *and spending all my money, honey*
> *and laughing at me like I was old Santa Claus.*
> *Well, someday you'll look and see*
> *I'm no longer there. Well darlin',*
> *just because, just because…*

And the kids listen, sometimes in small voices trying to sing along when they know some of the words. Mona drives quietly, but no sooner does Buzz's voice dive down into its final shakily held note than the next kid advances his plea for the country boy. The other still sees Santa Claus with his long white flowing beard and his red cap and his bright red rosy cheeks, sees his father somehow as Santa Claus, and hears the sound of someone laughing at him.

"Oh not that song," Mona demurs, shaking her head.

"Your mother doesn't want to hear that song," says Buzz, gazing around over the seat to the boys.

"Just once," says the kid. "You sang the other one," he implores.

Buzz turns to Mona, extending his hands, placing the proposition before her. She says, "Oh, all right," shaking her head. "Stupid song," she remarks as Buzz's voice comes out now stridently marching, the boy's voices joining in behind as they know the words to this one:

> Two Irishmen, two Irishmen, were diggin' in a ditch.
> One called the other one a dirty son-of-a...
> Peter Murphy, Peter Murphy, a little dog had he.
> He sent it to the neighbour to keep her company...

Buzz's head nods sharply in time with the rocking melody, the kids seeing the neighbour in the front room with the little dog, a framed painting on the wall and Mona now smiling as her high, quavering voice joins in with the song:

> She fed it, she fed it, she fed the little runt.
> It jumped up her petticoat and bit her on the count...
> ... ry boy, country boy, sitting on a rock.

The voices poise archly in the interval between the neighbour and the country boy, and in the kids' minds gaining anticipation as they approach their favourite part of the song:

> *Along came a bumblebee and stung him on the COCK …*
> *… tails, ginger ale, five cents a glass*
> *If ya don't like it, shove it up your ASS …*
> *… k me no more questions …*

The sheer daring of that part of the song causes them to surge with delight within, Buzz intoning the words defiantly as if nothing in the world could be more flagrant and derisive, then rising to the crescendo:

> *I'll tell you no more lies.*
> *If you ever get hit with a barrel of SHIT …*

Mona sings along with a kind of shrugging, bubbling camaraderie, as in "Hail, Hail, the Gang's All Here."

"Be sure to close your eyes!" the kids giggle with wide-eyed delight at the fiendish audacity of the final shameless "shit."

"Learned that one in the Navy," says Buzz, swigging from his beer and gazing out the window, smacking his lips contemplatively.

"Mom's turn to sing now," one of the boys pipes up.

Mona shakes her head. "No, it's not," she murmurs, driving.

"Ah, come on, Ma," says Buzz, his left arm stretching out along the top of the seat behind her. "Sing us a song," he croons.

"Yeah, Mom," the other kid insists.

"You guys always make fun of me," she pouts, half-serious, intent on the road.

"We won't make fun of ya," they say, and after a moment her voice timidly steps out on thin legs and tentatively tries the air…

> *On top of Old Smokey,*
> *all covered with snow…*

…careening off to the side with a lame wing, struggling to right itself in mid-air.

> *I lost my poor sweetheart*
> *for courting too slow…*

The last note falling lopsidedly away—Buzz winces comically…

> *For courting's a pleasure*
> *and parting is grief,*
> *but a false-hearted lover*
> *is worse than a thief*

Her voice unravels in the general area of the melody, swinging discordantly, dizzying itself and coasting to an uneasy stop.

"Well," Buzz sighs after a moment, "least you can't say you're any different than the rest of your family—they're all tone deaf as shit too." He smiles over at Mona, his hand on the back of her seat, reaching to touch her back.

✿

They pull into the driveway of George and Martha's, the dogs running up from the farmyard to bark them onto the property. "See ol' George finally got that shed fixed up," Buzz remarks, eyeing the freshly painted tractor shed by the side of the barn.

They pull up on the lawn by the front porch where several other cars have gathered. The dogs jump up yipping and yapping at them as they climb out of the car. Buzz yells, "Shaddap!" at them good-naturedly as Mona retrieves a cellophane-covered bowl of potato salad from the back seat and the kids tumble out. A plump ten-year-old girl comes tottering inquisitively from around behind the house.

"Hey Janey, how y'doin'?" Buzz greets her expansively. She looks up at him with wide white eyes. She's wearing cut-off blue jean shorts and carrying a long thin birch branch in her hand.

"What's the stick for?" one of the kids asks. Janey turns and looks wonderingly at the branch in her hand as if seeing it for the first time.

"She's playin' with it," Buzz explains, his eyes on the girl. "Could be a rifle, couldn't it—or anything, make a good putter, even eh?" he chuckles as Janey smiles and lazily swipes at the grass with the branch. The kids walk over to her and stand silently looking at the branch.

"Be a good bat, too," one of them says, as Buzz and Mona step onto the front porch, Mona ahead with the potato salad and Buzz following in through the screen door. The three children are left standing in the yard as the summer sun sets over the cornfield.

"Come in! Come in!" says George as they step into his front hall.

"Feel any different?" Mona says and smiles.

"Hell, no," George scoffs. "Bein' married twenty-five years is almost exactly like bein' married twenty-four, far as I can see." He kisses his sister on the cheek as Buzz observes, "Shit, George, you shouldn't be answerin' the door on your anniversary. What the hell, can't ya get anyone else out here to do that for ya?"

"Nope, Buzz, they all got their asses welded to their chairs in there," George remarks with brusque whimsy, his tiny eyes twinkling behind his spectacles, a middle-aged, prosperous farmer gentleman with thickening midriff and greying curly hair framing his pudgy face. The two men step into the kitchen as Mona sets the potato salad on a table laden with covered dishes and joins the other women sitting in the living room.

"I see they still haven't done nothin' about grading that road out there—Jesus, George, that's gotta be one of the worst roads in Shankton County!" exclaims Buzz, shaking his head. "Man! Just bump bump bump all the way in! I was sayin' on the way up here, when in hell're they gonna FIX this thing?"

George chuckles good-naturedly. "Well…" he begins.

"Who's in charge of that, anyhow?" Buzz asks. "That the town that owns that, or the county?"

"Well, Buzz," George explains, his voice drawling slowly as he gestures with his hands by the kitchen door, "apparently she's right on the line between Shankton County and Ursula, so what you have is the guy from Shankton County sayin' it's not their responsibility and the other guy from Ursula sayin' it ain't theirs, and ever' time election time comes up, why of course they both make sounds about it, and then of course after the election, nothin' gets done about it and another year goes by, and of course by then it's that much the worse."

"Jesus! No kiddin'!" asserts Buzz, shaking his head and wincing with distaste. "It's the worst goddamned road in Shankton County! You'd think they'd do something like in Point Linkton where with Mohawk Road they say, 'Well look, this sonofabitch runs right down the city line here, what we do is you pay half,' they say to the county, 'then we'll pay half.' And they get the damned thing paved and no one's gotta worry about it. I mean, that's the worst damn road in Shankton County!" Buzz says, jerking his thumb in the direction of the road.

"Mm-hm," George observes soberly. "What're you havin', Buzz?" he asks, moving to the fridge.

"Oh, just the usual," Buzz says nonchalantly, sitting down at the table. "Right, Elmer?" he asks the large jovial gentleman who's been sitting at the table, snickering with amusement at the byplay between George and Buzz.

"Right, Buzz, that's right," Elmer nods and chuckles, looking down with half-closed eyes at the bottle of beer he holds before him on the table.

"I mean, I nearly dislocate my backbone every time I ride that bastard in here," Buzz remarks, taking out his cigarette pack and lighting one as George sets a beer before him.

"How's it hangin' anyway, Elmer?" Buzz asks, blowing out a swift stream of smoke with which the flame of his match is extinguished.

"Oh, perty good, perty good, Buzz," Elmer replies, nodding his large head slowly, bringing his beer up for a quick pull, setting it on the table again, then wiping his mouth with the back of his hand. "Perty good, Buzz," he repeats quietly, looking down at the table with heavy-lidded eyes.

"How you doin', Russ?" Buzz asks another gentleman in a kitchen chair across the table from him.

"Doin' all right, Buzz, can't complain," replies Russ, a portly balding fellow leaning back, great, wiry, grey eyebrows over his merry, squinting eyes.

"That's right, 'cause no one listens anyway, right, Russ?" Buzz observes, winking at him conspiratorially.

"He he! You got that right, Buzz!" laughs Russ, nodding his head slowly and leaning further back in his chair, bringing his fingers up to tap the table. "That's fer sure!"

George stands leaning against the stove, his arms folded over his chest. "Don't know if you ever met ol' Uncle Zeb, Buzz, Martha's great-uncle on her father's side," he announces, gesturing with his beer bottle towards an elderly gentleman sitting on a chair in the corner behind Buzz.

"Nope I haven't," replies Buzz, turning with surprise. "Didn't even see him there," he chuckles, and all the men turn to see the old fellow sitting with his head bowed in the corner, his pale wrinkled fingers clutching a cane slanted across his knees.

"Hey! Zeb!" George calls to him.

"Sleepin' is he?" Buzz notes.

"Zeb!" George shouts. "Christ, he came down from Peaverton last Thursday, Buzz," he observes in a low murmur. "Can't do much else BUT sleep, far as I can see. Hey, ZEB!"

The old man's head slowly rises and he blinks confusedly. He works his jaw back and forth for a moment and he purses his lips. "Yep! Yep!" he croaks weakly. "We'll get 'er down there in a minute Chester!" he says then closes his eyes and his head slowly sinks back into its former position.

"Musta been out chasin' the women last night," Buzz remarks with a smile, and old Elmer beside him erupts in a low, deep-throated laugh, closing his eyes and throwing his head back. "Eh, Elmer?" Buzz grins, showing his white teeth.

"Musta' been, Buzz," Elmer agrees, nodding his head.

"Be doin' pretty good if he was," George observes soberly. "Old fella's eighty-six years old this July."

"Eighty-six. No shit, eh?" Buzz remarks, glancing appraisingly at the slumbering figure. "He's doin' all right, ain't he?"

"Well, I hope if I get to be that age and I'm like that," a slow grating voice pronounces from across the table, "somebody'll take me outside and SHOOT me!" It's ol' Harrison from down the road, a thin ruddy-faced farmer with dark, hard eyes, his knotty features clenched into a permanent sneer.

"Hey Bob, how're ya doin', anyway?" Buzz asks, pulling at his beer.

"I'm doin' all right, Buzz," ol' Harrison rasps in his low gravelly voice. "But if I'm ever like that over there," he says jerking his thumb in the direction of the sleeping figure in the corner, "I want ya to take me outside and SHOOT me!"

"No problem, Bob!" Buzz agrees affably. "I just gotta get my huntin' license renewed and we'll do 'er up right. Want me to use the twenty-two or would the ol' shotgun do the trick?" At this Elmer bursts forth in a new wave of hilarity, shaking his head from side to side.

"I'm SERIOUS," says ol' Henderson, gazing down the table bitterly. "Get old and fucked up like that ain't worth the trouble it takes to live, far's I'm concerned."

"Oh, I don't know," Russ offers. "You look at ol' Clarke out there on the fourth line. He was—what—seventy-six when he had a kid by that Elsie Schroeder, wasn't he?"

"Yep, yep, seventy-six or thereabouts," George agrees.

"Shit, that wouldn't be bad, if ya could pull off somethin' like that at that age, would it?" Russ remarks, shaking his head and clicking his tongue.

"Well, he musta been able to keep it up there and stiff for a few minutes, anyway, eh?" Buzz says as Elmer chuckles.

"Reminds me of that story of the ninety-seven-year-old guy with the young wife," Buzz continues, leaning forward. "Every time they went to bed at night the wife'd say, 'Now look you, you better be sure you don't get me knocked up! You be careful!'" Buzz relates, his eyes widening, his forefinger pointing emphatically, mimicking the woman's stern admonishment.

"And he'd say, 'Christ, woman, I'm ninety-seven years old! How in hell am I ever gonna get you knocked up! A man of my age!'" Buzz shouts, stretching out his hands, his voice rising with scorn and disbelief. "'There's no damn bullets in the gun anymore, lady!'"

All the men chuckle, now following Buzz's story with rapt attention, leaning forward, their mouths half-open.

"So one day she goes to the doctor and has a checkup," Buzz explains matter-of-factly. "The ol' doctor looks her over and then takes her aside. 'Madame,' he says, 'I must inform you that according to the tests I've performed, you are pregnant.'

"'Pregnant!' she says, 'Doctor, there is no way no possible way I could be pregnant!'

"'Madame,' the doctor says, 'this test is never wrong. I'm TELLING you you're pregnant.'

"'That's... that's impossible,'" says Buzz, stammering with the woman's befuddlement. "'Look, here, do that test again, something must've screwed up somewhere.'

"So the doctor comes back and says, 'Look, you're pregnant, there's no goddamned question about it, lady. You are PREGNANT!'"

Buzz pauses, shaking his head, taking a long swig from his beer while all around stare at him, listening, taut...

"So she says, 'JE-sus!' and goes over to the phone, phones up her husband and he answers and she says, 'Well, you old bastard, you went and got me knocked up!'" Buzz shouts accusingly, his eyes blinking angrily.

"And the old guy says," Buzz relates, squinting his eyes and blinking them perplexedly as he inquires into the phone he makes of his hand with pinky finger and forefinger extended, "'Excuse me, can I ask who's CALLING, please?'"

All the men pull back and erupt in a burst of laughter, slapping their knees and stamping their feet on the floor. George, standing by the door, throwing back his head and baring his teeth in a silent laugh, and Buzz grinning around at all of them as he chuckles, his eyes squeezed tight, almost closed in merriment.

"He had a couple others on the line, did he?" Russ remarks, smiling.

"She weren't the only one!" hoots George, and ol' Harrison at the end of the table nods his head and says, "Hmph!"

❂

A man with thick black hair, greying at the temples, appears at the kitchen door, looks around, and cries, "What the hell's goin' on in here?"

"Hey, Jack, how're you doin'?" George calls, and the man's ruddy face lights up with a bright smile as all the rest of the fellows turn to greet him. He enters, followed by his son Harley who lurches expressionlessly into the room and sprawls apathetically across a chair.

"I'm doin' all right, all right," Daddy Jack crows, waving in reply to the greetings as he takes a seat beside his son. "Had a devil of a time gettin' the warden out of the house as usual. By the time I'm all ready to go she ain't, or the other way around, or else we're both ready and in the car and half-way down the goddamned road and then she decides of course she's left somethin' back at home and we gotta turn around and get it, and by Jesus, she starts a-wailin' and I'm just glad we got here now anyways," he sighs, shaking his head.

"Don't suspect you'd say no to one of these here, then, would ye?" George asks, setting a beer before him.

"Nope, sure as hell wouldn't!" Daddy Jack smiles, picking up the beer and drinking deeply. "Course," Jack continues, smacking his lips, "don't take me too long to get ready anyway."

"Sure," Russ notes jocularly. "Just shit, shower and shave, right Jack?"

"That's right, Russ," Jack notes. "But the warden, well, she's like any woman and she's gotta fuss about fer a while, sure, but after that it's the other waitin' that gets me, and then her comin' out after she's dressed herself and wantin' me to change MY clothes!"

"She's gotta dress you too, does she?" Russ laughs.

"Oh, Christ, yes!" Daddy Jack yells. "And then with this, that, and the other thing, and what she's remembered or forgot, and of course you can't say a word to 'er 'cause she gets in such a state."

"She gets a bit testy, does she, Jack?" Buzz asks, grinning.

"Oh, Christ!" Jack replies, shaking his head and wincing as if in physical pain. "Christ, yes!"

"How you doin', there, Elmer?" Jack calls out above the general laughter.

"I'm doin' all right, all right, Jack," Elmer replies, nodding and slowly blinking his heavy-lidded eyes.

"I don't believe I saw ya since that trouble you had last month," Jack continues, his voice several decibels louder than necessary. "Stroke, wasn't it?"

"Yep, yep, a little one," Elmer nods, looking down at his hands. "Took a little bit outta me, though."

"Suspect it would! I suppose they got ya on more pills than ya could count!" Jack observes.

"Yeah, somethin' like that," Elmer says, smiling slightly as he brings his beer to his lips.

"Just like when I had that kidney trouble there three years ago," Jack exclaims. "They give ya pills to take in the morning, at night, pills after you shit, before you shit. Christ—it's enough to drive ya crazy!"

"That's right, Jack," Elmer chuckles.

"And then they want ya to keep comin' in till—HEY!" Jack shouts, turning to his son. "Put that down!"

Harley lifts Jack's beer to his mouth and drinks defiantly.

"I said put it down!" Jack shouts.

"Ah, keep your shirt on," Harley mutters, disdainfully placing the beer on the table.

"I tol' you before to leave that alone!" Jack says angrily.

"You said before I could have ONE," Harley insists.

"I didn't say anything like it!" Jack cries. "Don't you get goddamn lippy with me or you can walk your ass outta here and right on home!"

Harley settles back in his chair and looks scornfully off at the distant wall. "Bull-SHIT!" he sneers.

"I'll bullshit you!" Jack shouts, infuriated. "You shouldn't even be here anyhow—you should be at home helpin' Bud with the chores!" Jack turns to the other men. "This little beggar can get outta more work than anyone I ever knew!"

"Doesn't like to work, eh, Jack?" Buzz asks.

"Shit! He gets outta more work than anybody I ever saw!" Jack fumes, glaring resentfully at his son, who stares sullenly off into the distance. "Anytime any chores to be done or work goin' on at all and this guy disappears into thin air!"

"Yeah right!" Harley snorts, his arms folded across his chest, his foot tapping the floor impatiently.

"Well, the answer to that, Jack, I would say, is maybe a bit more discipline on the way up," George observes, tipping his head back to swallow a long draught of beer.

"I tried, George, I tried!" Jack insists, "but it's his mother that's the problem, she gets this guy off the hook and coddles 'im like he was still a little baby time after time! Anytime I try to lay down the law, why, his mother steps in and wrecks it all!"

"Well, all's I know," George offers laconically, "is that if I ever tried any of that kind of business when I was that age, my old man would've cuffed me upside the head into the middle of next week quicker 'n shit through a goose."

"Same as mine, same as mine!" Jack agrees passionately, nodding his head with vigour. "Mine would've too!" he cries, as the other men likewise voice their agreement and Harley surveys the wall and with an aristocratic air of disdain snorts, "Pah!"

"What mighty problems of the world are you all tryin' to solve now?" a middle-aged, grey-haired woman inquires as she sashays in through the door.

"Oh, we haven't even got to the heavy stuff yet!" Russ observes jovially.

"Just warmin' up, are yous?" Maxine asks as she moves to the sink, pouring a glass of water.

"You know us," George remarks. "What can I get for ya, here?"

"Oh, nothing at all," Maxine says, turning with the glass. "I'm just doin' my nursing duties," she explains with a smile, laying three tablets on the table before Elmer. "If I don't administer 'em to him, he'll never remember to take 'em," she explains, gazing fondly down at her husband.

Elmer picks up the pills and grudgingly places them in his mouth, his thin lips prissily opening and closing over them, his long face dull with tired resignation as he takes the glass of water.

"Goin' down all right, Elmer?" Buzz asks with a tenuous jocularity as he watches Elmer pour the water down his throat, his head cocked back and his Adam's apple bobbing. Maxine places her hand on her husband's shoulder as he sets the glass down and looks up at her expressionlessly.

"Needs a shot of some good scotch to do it up right, eh, Elmer?" Buzz grins, and Elmer manages a slight wry smile.

"He doesn't need anything of the kind!" Maxine says as she breezes back to the sink. "He hates those pills like the devil, though—wish there was something we could do to make 'em easier to take."

"Goddamn things," Elmer mutters, leaning forward and resting his elbows on the table, looking down grimly.

"Well you're just going to have to take those 'goddamned things' till you're better and the doctor says you don't have to take them anymore!" Maxine remonstrates, nodding her head sharply with each word, standing by the counter with her hands on her hips.

Elmer raises his head slightly and looks sideways at Buzz, a look of grim misery and plaintive resignation so unguarded in his eyes that Buzz gulps, shakes his head and clicks his tongue, saying in effect, "Bugger, ain't it?"

❂

"I'll be back in another three-quarters of an hour," Maxine says as she walks past Jack and Harley bickering heatedly in low voices and out through the kitchen door into the living room where Momma Simpson sits with Mona. George's wife Martha sits on the couch silently knitting as Bess Armstrong from down the road tells them all about the McMurphys' divorce, how for three years Flo McMurphy had been telling Bob she was going clog dancing but really going out and meeting Bert Hardy at Pendleton, twenty miles away so's nobody'd see 'em.

Old Bob sitting at home watching television didn't suspect a thing till one day at the bank Bob met Elma Norton and they got to talking and he asked her how the clogging was going, so of course Elma said they hadn't been having classes for a year by that time.

Well, that got Bob to thinking, so that Wednesday night Bob was lyin' there watching television and when Flo came in Bob asked, "So how was the clogging tonight?"

And Flo said it was just fine, had a real good time and what have you, and Bob looked up from the television and asked her who was there, and Flo says, oh, Bernice Finley and Elma and Jeanette and the rest, kind of wondering now since this was the first time he'd ever really asked about her clog dancing—even when she really did go to clog dancing—but he just turned back to the television anyway and just said "Mm-hm," and then nothing else was said.

She just forgot about it, and the next Wednesday she went off as usual, sayin' goodbye as she went out and leavin' him there watchin' television. But what she didn't know was that about one half-minute after she shut the door he was off that couch and on his feet, walking out through the kitchen to the back where he'd parked Jimmy McPherson's car which he'd borrowed from work that day, and he got in that car and followed her right down Main Street and down the highway to Pendleton—her not knowing or even suspecting 'cause after all it'd been three years—right into the parking lot of the diner off the highway on the outskirts of Pendleton where they'd meet, and he watched her get out of the car and walk in and greet Bert Hardy.

Bob sat in his car and watched through the window as she

held hands with Bert Hardy and had coffee for twenty minutes, and watched them as they got up and left for wherever
they went off to, and he just said to himself, "Mm-hm," then
turned around and drove home.

So that night when she comes home he just lays there in
front of the TV, doesn't even bother asking her how the clogging was, and she just goes off and gets ready for bed as usual.
And then a week goes by and the next Wednesday she goes
off again as usual, leavin' him there on the couch. She drives
to Pendleton and walks into the diner, her pace pickin' up as
she walks up to the table to see Bert, and there sittin' in their
special booth right across from Bert is Bob!

What happened is that Bob scooted off that couch right
after she left and drove hell bent for election down the backroads to Pendleton and got there before she did! And there's
Bert lookin' at her all in a panic and Bob's just smilin' at her
like nothin' would melt in his mouth, with a coffee in front of
him, and sayin' all calm, "Have a seat, Flo."

Well I don't know if you could've written too big a book
about what was goin' on in her mind then! So not knowing
what to do, she kinda stumbles over and sits down, looking at
Bob in a daze, her heart pounding, wondering what on earth
he's gonna do.

And of course Bert Hardy's probably wondering that too,
knowing Bob won that middleweight wrestling badge back in
high school and Bert himself just a little thin slip of a guy. But
Bob just sits there smiling at them, his mouth smiling a calm
smile but his eyes not smiling at all, just bright and sparkling
and still and fixed on them, and not saying anything, which
scared Flo even more till she just wished to God he would

begin shouting and turning over the table.

And it seemed like three hours till Bob finally said in a calm, friendly voice, "Well, it's gonna be Christmas soon, and Christmas is a time for beautiful things to happen." He pauses and looks at them for about a minute with that same awful smile. "Now, Bert, I've looked after Flo here for seventeen years, so I suppose it's your turn to take over." He reaches down into his pocket and pulls out a set of car keys and puts them on the table. "These are Jimmy McPherson's car keys—I borrowed his car to come out here. Now if you can have it back in his driveway by seven in the morning, and I can get the keys back to my car so I can drive home, we can just call ourselves even," he says, looking at Flo, his eyes boring into her.

Flo fumbles in her purse and takes out the keys and puts them on the table.

Bob picks them up and puts them in his pocket, saying "Thanks a lot," then gets out of the booth. "Have a good Christmas," he says as he starts walking away.

All of a sudden in a weak voice Flo says, "Bob…" and Bob turns around just as quick, raising his hand.

"Christmas is a time for beautiful things to happen," he says. Then he goes to the cash register, pays for his coffee, wishin' a Merry Christmas to the waitress, then walks on out, gets into his car and pulls out of the driveway of the diner.

"Hm!" says Maxine after a moment. "Well, one thing anyway, that Flo McMurphy never had any problem gettin' what she wanted anyhow, once she decided what it was."

"That's true enough," says Bess Armstrong, taking a swig from her screwdriver. "I remember hearin' stories about her out on the backroads with her pants around her ankles when I was a teenager and I never did believe 'em, but I can't say I don't believe 'em now!"

"Oh, pssshhh," Mona laughs in a light mocking manner. "If all Bob McMurphy ever did was sit in front of that TV night after night, why you can't blame Flo getting a bit bored. And besides, that Bert Hardy was probably getting lonely himself. His mother died last year, didn't she?" She squints her eyes, looking around at the others inquisitively.

"She did," Momma Grace Simpson attests. "Cancer. She had a long, hard time of it—and ol' Bert, he'd be in there every day, always bringin' in something for her." She looks off into the distance, shaking her head as she leans forward, resting her plump elbows on her knees. "Two of 'em were close as close could be. Near the end he had 'em put a cot in her room so he could sleep there, just so he could bring her some comfort. And of course he could hardly bring himself to be apart from her, that's how close they were."

"Well, that's the most surprising thing about it, if you ask me," offers Bess Armstrong. "That it would be Bert Hardy. Can't say he'd be my first choice if I was out on the loose."

"Oh, I don't know," Maxine interjects. "He must have some money hidden away, what with old Ma Hardy's way of holding onto a dollar." She looks slyly around at all the women and they chuckle.

"That's true," agrees Bess Armstrong, laughing—then looking down solemnly at her screwdriver. "But nobody'd ever think, would they, that Bert Hardy, or PeeWee as they used to call him, would be the kind to break up a home, him workin' there in the library and livin' all those years with his mother; kinda fella would soon as run away as talk to ya, it seemed," she says, shaking her head. "Just a spindly little guy."

"Oh, break up a home," Mona scoffs whimsically. "Sounds to me like there wasn't much of a home to break up in the first place."

"Well, whatever," says Bess Armstrong, waving her hand. "All's I know is ever since then ol' Bob McMurphy's been in O'Toole's practically every night closin' the place down, moanin' to everyone who'll listen about losing Flo and how much he loves her, and everything else."

"A little too late for that now, I think," Mona observes, looking abstractedly across the couch beside her to Martha Simmons, who sits quietly knitting, her white-haired head bowed intently to the task. Mona smiles at Martha's absorbed face in profile. "What do you think, Martha?" she asks her sister-in-law after a moment.

Martha looks up suddenly, turning with some surprise. "What?" she asks, her tired eyes blinking behind her spectacles. "I'm sorry," she says, chuckling along with Mona's laughter and looking back to her handiwork. "I guess I wasn't listening, I was so caught up in this."

"Is Nia going to be coming tonight?" Mona asks, gazing at her fondly.

"Well yes, she's supposed to be, but whether they've been held up on the highway or not, I'm not sure," says Martha, her eyes narrowing as she stares down with some concern at her knitting. "That fellow Webb, her new beau, is supposed to be bringing her."

"Oh yes, he came with her to Judy's wedding, didn't he?" Mona remarks.

"Mm-hm," Martha murmurs, considering a problem in her knitting, then working at it anew, her fingers moving dexterously with the needles. "Er, yes," she says, knitting, turning to Mona briefly. "She did."

COME ALL YE YOUNG LOVERS (II)

WEBB AND NIA DRIVE DOWN THE DARKENED COUNTRY road—Webb a young gentleman of thirty-four years of age, balding in the area of the forehead, spidery strands of his dark hair stretching forth in an ineffectual attempt to make up for it. For similar purposes, a wiry black beard covers his jawline, chin and mouth. His tiny eyes blink behind thick, silver-framed spectacles.

Nia, a slender petite young woman at his side, has short golden hair. She's dressed in a sweater and blue jeans and sits staring silently at the road before her, elfin features as blank as an empty sheet of paper.

Webb looks over to this face with increasing frequency, stealing uneasy glances, his eyes darting from the road to her profile; he's concerned that they haven't exchanged words for the past fifteen minutes. With each successive moment of silence, his distress increases: he casts about in his mind for a phrase to unlock the stalemate, and biting his lip worriedly, he succumbs, reaching down to turn the radio on, calling forth its static and murmur to fill the car.

Nia sighs and after a moment, still considering the road, she asks, "Why'd you turn on the radio?"

He looks at her blankly then reaches down to adjust the tuner. "I just wanted to check the hockey scores," he says quickly. "Last night's game."

"Hm," she says. "I didn't know you were so deeply into hockey."

"I'm... not," he stutters nervously, looking over at her quickly as he fiddles with the tuner knob. "It's just that the guys at the office have a pool going, and I made a bet."

"I see," she says, turning and smiling at him, taking in his fretful expression, his frowning mouth half-hidden beneath his black muff of a beard. "I thought maybe you just turned on the radio because we haven't had anything much to say to each other for the last forty-five minutes," she observes.

He chuckles, shaking his head. "No!" he laughs. "I don't know why you'd think that. I just wanted to get the score," he says, finally getting the news on the radio. After several moments the sports comes on. Nia watches with amusement as Webb listens intently, his face a mask of studious absorption. "All right," he says, nodding his head once quickly, reaching down to turn the radio off.

"Did you get the information you needed?" she asks him.

"Yes, I did," he replies.

"Well?"

"Well what?" he asks, somewhat testily.

"Well, did you win or lose?" she asks, her eyes flashing with mischief.

"Oh—lost," he says, shrugging, watching the road with grim stoicism.

"That's the way it goes, I guess, eh?" she remarks, smiling.

"Yep," he says and nods. And in an attempt at nonchalance, he begins to make a clicking sound with his tongue against the roof of his mouth.

She erupts in a sudden burst of laughter and reaches over to pull playfully at his beard. "When you gonna shave this thing off, huh?" she asks, giggling.

He begins to visibly redden all around the area of his cheeks and across his sizable forehead where his hairline recedes and gives way to the feeble sparseness of the thin hairs clinging for dear life. He purses his lips, then smiles in spite of himself. "Hey, look out, I'm trying to drive here, okay?" he says, his voice wavering.

She tugs on his beard again, then moves her tiny hand over to massage the back of his neck: he squirms beneath her cool fingers in a mixture of pleasure and embarrassment. "Oh, is that right?" she asks. "Is Mr. Serious trying to drive right now?"

He coughs, furrowing his brow. "So… who's gonna be at this thing, anyhow?"

She takes her hand off his neck, reclining her petite body and resting her foot on the dashboard, sighing, "All the usuals." She looks listlessly out the side window. "A lot of the same ones that were at Judy's wedding."

"Hm," he says. He cranes his neck and looks over his shoulder, turning from the paved road onto a bumpy gravel road. "Will Raymond be there?" he asks, glancing at her sideways with a touch of apprehension.

"Oh, probably," Nia says then turns and looks at him cunningly. "You don't like him, do you?"

"Who?"

"Raymond," she laughs, rolling her eyes. "After what happened at the wedding."

He squints at the road, compressing his mouth. "What happened at the wedding?" he asks.

"Oh, okay," she says, staring out the window. "All right."

Webb frowns, biting his lower lip. He drums his fingers against the steering wheel and exhales a long exasperated breath.

"I don't know why you say I don't like him," he blurts out irritatedly. "He was just there at the wedding and I …"

"You're going to miss the turnoff!" Nia announces, straightening up in her seat and pointing. "It's this road here!"

The car is clumsily brought to a sudden halt, Webb twisting around in his seat to back it up. They turn off onto the road, the car bumping and jiggling up and down on its shocks over the rough gravel. "Jesus, what a rough road!" Webb exclaims. Nia giggles and indicates the farm a distance down the road, the house all lit up with golden light in every window and an assemblage of cars parked helter-skelter all over the front lawn.

"Sure a lot of people here," Webb notes as they pull in the laneway.

"Yeah," says Nia distractedly as they ease down the long drive, the dogs suddenly appearing out of the darkness to yelp and run around the car.

"What's with these dogs?" Webb notes, squinting out the window at them in puzzlement.

"Why don't you just drop me off at the door, here," Nia suggests, "and park the car?"

He looks at her questioningly as he stops the car and she opens the door, jumping out. "Where should I park?" he calls after her.

"Anywhere!" she laughs back over her shoulder as she slips out into the cooling summer night. "Then come on in!"

Webb sits in the car and watches her slide across the lawn and onto the porch of the house, sees the screen door open and friendly arms reach out to greet her in. He grunts "Hmph!" as he motors the car slowly across the lawn to the side of the house and gets out. The dogs rush tumbling and leaping up to him, barking and yelping, and he starts back, a bit panicked.

"Get out! Get away!" he shouts, waving his arms at them. The dogs content themselves with standing directly in front of him and barking happily up at his face in response. "Git!" he says angrily, stamping his foot and accompanying his command with a fluttering gesture of his fingers, when he suddenly turns and becomes aware of three small children standing in the shadows at the side of the house, staring at him.

"Hello," he greets them, smiling, feeling his face and his forehead grow warm with embarrassment.

The three children stare up at him, three white faces in the night, with wide expressionless eyes.

"Out here playing, are you?" Webb asks, nodding and grinning, the lights from the windows of the house sparkling on the rims of his spectacles.

The children stare at him for a long moment, as if carefully taking his full measure, before turning in unison and mutely trudging off around the side of the house.

Webb grunts, his embarrassment changing swiftly to anger, and he stomps ahead, the dogs parting to each side of him, continuing in their intrepid barking and yelping, circling his shoes and looking merrily up at him.

"Goddamn," he mutters, knocking on the screen door.

"Come on in!" a voice cries out. "Ya don't hafta knock!"

He pulls open the door and stumbles into the front hall, then turns and peeks around the corner into the living room: an assemblage of middle-aged women sit about on the over-stuffed chairs and on the couch, all staring at him in sudden silence, holding their drinks poised in mid-air—some of them blinking with searching curiosity.

"Well, there he is!" one of the women pipes up, and all the women laugh as Bess Armstrong leaps up, rushes to him, throws her arms around his neck, pulls his flinching, squinting face to hers and gives him a loud, smacking kiss full on the mouth.

"How ya doin', honey?" she shouts as the other women guffaw heartily. Mona Hendricks calls out above them, "Hello, Webb!"

"Hello, Aunt Mona," Webb says, nodding and blinking in confusion as Bess stands beside him with her arm reaching up and around his neck and grins broadly at the ladies.

"Tall one, ain't he?"

"Is Nia around?" Webb asks, raising his voice slightly to be heard over the general laughter.

"She just went to the washroom," Mona informs him, smiling from across the room.

"Like to keep tabs on her every minute, don't ya?" Bess shouts, pulling him closer. "Well, ain't that cute! Well, she's otherwise indisposed in the POWDER room right now, sweetie!" Bess pulls his head down and brings her face close to his.

"Oh, Bess!" Maxine laughs, leaning back in her chair.

"Martha, Webb's here," Mona says softly to Martha Simmons, sitting beside her on the couch.

"Pardon?" Martha asks, looking up from her knitting.

"Webb," Mona says, pointing to him.

"Oh, yes," Martha says, smiling faintly. "Hello, Webb," she says, nodding, then returns to her knitting.

"Hi, Martha," Webb smiles nervously.

"Well, honey, as you can see," Bess says in a loud whisper, "there ain't nothin' but a bunch of us old broads out here in the front room. Whyn't you go out in the kitchen where all the menfolk are and get yourself a beer?" she says, patting him softly on the rump.

"Uh, yes," he mutters with some embarrassment, hearing the chuckles of the women all around him, and turning toward the kitchen where he hears the loud, hoarse voices of the men talking and laughing. He steps toward the kitchen with some trepidation, his self-consciousness weighting his limbs until it seems a great effort to him to extricate himself from the room. Bess's hand suddenly shoots forth, grabbing him tightly by the wrist and bringing him stumbling back to her.

"There's gonna be a dance later in the garage," she slurs in a deep whisper, her mouth warm and wet at his ear, "and you're gonna be my partner. We're gonna dance the first dance of the night—is that right?" she asks.

"Yeah, yeah, sure," Webb answers nervously, attempting to pull his wrist from her grip.

"All right," Bess murmurs conspiratorially, finally releasing him and patting him again on his buttocks as he stumbles through the doorway into the kitchen where all the men are in the midst of laughing at an unheard joke, leaning back in their chairs and hooting, some snickering and shaking their heads and looking down at the table. Buzz is at the centre of it all, looking around from face to face with eyes squinted tight with amusement.

❋

Webb attempts to slide into the room as inconspicuously as possible, making his way against the wall and heading towards the counter, but as the laughter subsides all the men one by one turn to gaze at him with a questioning stare, their smiles disappearing from their faces.

"Hello," Webb says shyly, standing awkwardly by the counter.

They all nod, once, grimly. "How y'doin'?" some say.

"Now, who's that?" cries Uncle George as he comes stomping in the door, off the back of the kitchen, carrying three beers in each hand from the back-porch fridge. "Ah, it's Nia's new husband!" he grunts, placing the beers on the counter and reaching forth to grasp Webb's hand. "Or soon to be, anyway!" he chuckles. "Well, do ya know everyone here?"

"Hi, George," says Webb, clasping George's hand with

relief and looking about the room. "I think I remember some of them from Judy's wedding…"

"Well let me give you a little tour of Mug's Gallery here," George says, drawing himself up and extending his hand to the men.

"Yeah, comin' from the biggest mug of them all!" Buzz remarks, winking at Webb as Elmer at his side bends his head and closes his eyes, snickering.

"All right, all right," says George, somewhat annoyed. "The smartass there is Buzz. You probably remember him from the wedding."

"Yes," says Webb, nodding. "Hello, Buzz."

"Hiya, partner, how're ya doin'?" Buzz grins, winking roguishly.

"And that guy there beside him is Elmer, Nia's uncle. You more 'n likely to remember him too," George explains.

"Oh yes, hello, Elmer!" Webb smiles with a half-wave.

Elmer pulls his beer from his lips with a smack, places it on the table and swallows his mouthful with a quiet gulping noise. "H'lo!" he says with a slight nod of his head.

"And this right here is Russ, Nia's other uncle. You prob'ly remember him too," says George.

"Yes. Hello, Uncle Russ!" Webb smiles, waving.

Russ grins brightly, his eyes sparkling as he shows his bright white teeth. "G'day!" he shouts.

"And that ol' geezer over there is Ol' Bob Harrison from down the road, an ol' friend of the family, I don't know if you ever met him before," says George, indicating Harrison, who sits leaning back from the table with a sullen scowl on his face, his arms folded across his chest, surveying the room with disdain.

"Hello, Bob!" Webb says gamely, smiling, and Ol' Harrison's eyes squint as he looks up and slowly focuses them on Webb. His mouth tightens into an even more unforgiving sneer as he exhales a swift, even breath through his nostrils, piercing Webb through with a cold glare of hostility.

"And that guy over there is... oh, hell!" George exclaims. "I ain't gonna introduce 'em all!" he says, throwing up his hands. "You'll get to know 'em all soon enough anyhow. Anyway, what'll you have, Webb? We ain't got none of them fancy drinks here like you might get in the big city, but we got beer, and we got..."

"Oh, a beer will be fine," Webb says quickly, finding a space along the counter to lean against.

"Okey-dokey, sir, comin' right up!" George sings out, turning to grab the beer. As Webb stands still recovering from the fierce glare of Ol' Harrison, he feels himself being sharply observed by a figure on his left. Slowly and with some trepidation, he turns and looks down and sees the mocking face of Harley staring at him from where he sits sprawled in a kitchen chair. Webb sees the stringy, long blond hair, cheeks besieged with glistening pimples and the hard, glittering eyes.

"Hello, Harley," Webb says amiably, attempting a convivial smile as Harley surveys him from head to toe, his lips twitching with secret amusement, then looks him in the eyes scornfully for a moment before snorting, "Pah!" and turning away disgustedly.

"Now listen, listen to this one, Elmer," Buzz is saying to Elmer, laying his hand on Elmer's arm as George gives Webb his beer.

"Listen to me," Buzz says seriously, leaning closer to Elmer as if to convey to him a message of the utmost importance. "Are ya listenin'? Now listen: there was this guy, see, who was cheap as the devil…"

The other men in the room turn and look at Buzz, half-smiling with expectation, hearing the stridency of his voice. "Damn cheap he was, the cheapest bastard in the whole wide world," Buzz explains, shaking his head and grimacing. "And he had all this money, too, he was rich, he was a millionaire for Christ's sake, and he wouldn't buy his wife NOTHIN'. Nothin'! He was a no-good cheap sonofabitch!" Buzz pronounces emphatically, looking around the room, as if daring anyone to dispute what he's saying.

"Now his wife, of course, she's just like any woman, she wants to have some nice clothes, and a nice place to live, and flowers and all that shit, you know. But this guy is CHEAP! Goddamn it he's cheap! He makes her live in a rundown dump that a dog wouldn't shit in, he drives a car that's thirty years old and is fallin' apart, and he makes her wear old clothes that are fulla holes—fuckin' rags is what she's got to wear, practically, and she's miserable as hell."

The men nod and chuckle. "So anyways, one day they're drivin' down the highway and they see this big, beautiful, beautiful lakefront house for sale. Three storeys… a balcony over the lake, a fireplace. Just beautiful…"

He pauses a moment to savour the beauty of the house, shaking his head from side to side reverently and taking a long drag off his cigarette. He sets the cigarette down, blowing out a gust of smoke as he speaks.

"And so she says, 'You got lots a money, a million dollars,

for Christ's sake. You bastard, why don't you buy that house? The one we got now is fallin' to pieces.'

"And he turns and says, 'Piss off, I ain't buyin' you no new damn house. The one we got now's just fine.'

"Well, she grumbles and complains and bitches, and they drive along and all of a sudden the car starts breakin' down a bit, makin' all these goddamn noises and actin' up. Practically stalls right there on the highway, so she turns to him and says, 'You old cheapskate, when the hell are you gonna buy a new car?'

"And he says, "Look—you can shut your trap right now 'cause one thing I can tell ya, I… ain't… buyin'… YOU… no… new… damn… car!' And, Jesus, the car's fallin' apart! It's a wreck! But he won't buy a car! God—DAMN!" Buzz exclaims, looking around in disbelief.

"So they're drivin' on and on, and they pass this fur store, this store for furs down the road, with, you know, mink and rabbit and whatever the hell. So she says, 'You know what I want? I want a brand new, damn mink coat!'

"He says, 'I'm NOT gonna buy you no fuckin' mink coat.'

"She says, 'Well, why the hell not?'

"And he says, 'I am NOT gonna buy you no mink coat so you can just forget about it. Piss off!' Now, imagine that! Guy's got all this money and he won't buy her nothin'! He was a mean, cheap, rotten bastard!"

Buzz pauses to shake his head with deep disapproval.

"So finally… they're drivin' along and all of a sudden she turns to him and says, 'You mean, cheap, old bastard, take off your pants—I wanna give you a blow job!'

"He looks at her and says, 'Screw that! You ain't gonna

give me no blow job! You ain't gonna 'cause I ain't gonna let ya! So forget about it! Screw that!'

"He's so cheap now," Buzz cries, pounding the table with his fist and looking around at everyone with an expression of pained exasperation, "…he's so goddamned cheap he won't even give his own wife the pleasure of givin' him a blow job!"

Buzz nonchalantly takes a swig of his beer as he gives his grinning audience a moment to digest this information.

"So one day," he says, smacking his lips, "not long after that, the guy dies. He just takes a big bastard of a heart attack one day, keels over and dies just like that. So first thing the wife does, naturally, is gets ahold of all his money, all the so many millions of dollars he's got. She takes his money and the first thing she does is have him cremated and has him put in this little cardboard box, neat as can be.

"She takes the box and she goes out to a car lot and she says, 'All right you bastard, watch this: you wouldn't buy me a new car when I asked ya, but now I'm gonna buy the most expensive fuckin' thing I can find, and with your money! And there's nothin' you can do about it!' She buys the most expensive car on the lot! The most expensive one! A giant car with six doors and all the accessories you can imagine.

"She puts the cardboard box on the seat beside her and roars on down the highway, just givin' 'er, one hundred miles an hour, and she screeches up in fronta the mink store, and she says, 'All right, take a look at this, cheapskate, I'm goin' in there and I'm gonna get that fur coat I wanted and there's nothin' you can do about it!' She waltzes in, buys the biggest damn mink coat you ever saw, puts it on and comes traipsin' right on back out again.

Jumps in the car and says, 'How do you like THAT, cheap-skate?' And burns it right on down to that beautiful house—it so happens there's a real estate agent standin' right out in front. She looks down at the cardboard box and says, 'Oh you bastard, I hope you're watching this!' She strolls up and buys that house just like that—cash!" Buzz says, snapping his fingers. "She takes the box, goes into the house, walks up the stairs and goes out to the balcony. She opens up the box and dumps all the ashes over this big table there.

"She looks down at the ashes and says, 'Okay, bastard, I asked you time after time for a new car but you were too goddamn cheap to buy one. I got the car now, the biggest, most expensive one I could find. You were too damn cheap to ever buy me a new mink coat—I got one now, and there's nothin' you can do about it! For thirty years we lived in a broken-down shack you wouldn't even spend money on to fix up and you wouldn't even think about buyin' a new house—well, here I am now sittin' in this mansion that I bought with your money and I hope it's drivin' you nuts! All your life you were so damned cheap and mean you wouldn't even give me the pleasure of givin' you a blow job!'" Buzz says, growing almost breathless with the telling of his tale.

"'And now, by God, so help me, I'm gonna give it to ya!' So she leans over the pile of ashes there and she goes…" Buzz leans forth and blows a brisk stream of air through his puckered lips over the table, "Ppptttwwwhhh!"

❁

All the men burst into riotous laughter: Jack throwing his head back and closing his eyes; George standing by the counter and grinning broadly, shaking his head slowly from side to side; Elmer looking up at the ceiling, his shoulders shaking.

"Heh, heh, she finally got to do it, eh?" Russ chuckles as the laughter reaches its peak.

"Never heard that one before, eh?" Buzz is asking the still-shaking Elmer as a slight, meek, little woman appears cautiously at the doorway of the kitchen.

"George," Aunt Martha calls, her knitting in her hand. "George! When you gonna come out and open the presents all these nice people gave us?"

George's wild laughter ceases and an expression of irritated distaste comes slashing across his features. "Why don't you hold your goddamned horses?" he shouts. "We got plenty of time! I'll be out there when I'm ready!" In the quick silence of the room all the men stare uncomfortably at the floor as Aunt Martha shifts the knitting in her hand and blinks her small tired eyes.

"Well... I just wanted to know!" she pronounces with a sharp nod of her grey head as she turns and leaves.

"Jesus!" George mutters, turning to the fridge to replace his beer, and several of the men chuckle.

"Still likes to keep a good tab on ya, does she George?" Russ grins, and George grunts sullenly as he pops open his new beer.

"Well, that's somethin' anyhow," Buzz observes. "Good to see she's still carin' where you're at anyhow after twenty-five years, eh?"

As the men voice their amusement at this latest observation, Webb smiles, raising his beer to his lips. As he does so, he suddenly notices Ol' Harrison at the far end of the table, staring intently at him and frowning, squinting his eyes in apparent puzzlement. Webb turns away for a moment then looks uneasily over at him again, meeting the same absorbed, dissatisfied gaze.

"And what is it that you do?" the slow, gravelly drawl inquires from the end of the table. A sudden sting of cold sweat breaks out at Webb's hairline.

"Pardon?" he asks, his grin frozen on his face.

"What is it you do," Ol' Harrison rasps, nodding toward him, "for a living?"

"Oh, he's a phot-aww-grapher!" a mocking voice pipes up—Harley, grinning sardonically up at Webb from his chair.

"Yes," Webb explains nervously to Ol' Harrison. "I'm a photographer."

"A photographer! Hm!" Ol' Harrison notes, and whistles in mock surprise. He leans forward and folds his hands before him on the table. "A photographer! Now… and you do that for a living?" he asks seriously, cocking his head to one side and regarding Webb with stern eyes.

"Yes, yes I do," Webb says, feeling the silence in the room around him, all of the men now following the exchange.

"And you make your living by that, you go around taking pictures for a living?" Ol' Harrison says argumentatively, squinting his eyes incredulously as if the idea is so fantastic he can't conceive of it.

"Yes," Webb answers almost apologetically, feeling all eyes upon him.

Ol' Harrison closes his eyes, picks up his beer, and bends

his head back to take a long sucking swallow. He pulls the bottle from his mouth with a smacking noise and peers at Webb again, still dissatisfied.

"SO," he grunts, "what is it that you take pictures of?"

"Oh," Webb stutters, "weddings and babies…"

Harley starts snickering loudly at his side.

Ol' Harrison glares at Webb for a long moment as if trying torturously to come to some conclusion in his mind. Then, suddenly, unexpectedly, he starts to smile, showing his teeth in an amused grin. He looks around the room, chuckling. "Weddings and babies," he mutters, raising his open palm in Webb's direction. "Shit!" he groans, shaking his head from side to side and staring down at the floor. "Weddings and *babies*!" he mutters.

"You'll have to excuse Ol' Harrison, Webb," Buzz notes with a grin. "The only photography he's been acquainted with are the pictures on the top of the hardware store calendar. Ain't that right, Bob?"

But Ol' Harrison stares bitterly at the table before him, his face fixed in a resentful scowl.

"I saw some of his pictures—Martha showed me 'em!" Harley volunteers, looking about the room.

Webb turns, surprised. "You did?" he asks quietly.

"Yeah!" Harley says looking up at him, his eyes flashing maliciously, lips pressed together in a smirk. "And I thought they stank like shit!" he announces.

Webb stands mortified, a cold wave of embarrassment washing over him.

"Harley, you shut up!" Daddy Jack explodes. "You ain't so smart! You don't know nothin' about photography!"

"Yeah, like you do!" Harley retorts with a laughing sneer.

"You shut up! You ain't so smart!" Jack shouts, his face reddening with his anger. "Damn smartass is what he is!" he says, looking around the room at all the other men.

"Yep, that's right, Jack, that's what he is," George observes, frowning down at the insolent, disdainful teenager with grim disapproval. "He's a goddamned smartass is what he is." He studies Harley decisively as he raises his beer to his lips. "Needs a week out here on my farm. We'd shape 'im up perty good, I bet," he says, taking a short drink, then turning suddenly to Webb. "Hey Webb, I don't think you ever met Ol' Uncle Zeb yet, did ya?"

Webb stares at George for a moment, stunned. "Oh no, no I haven't," he stutters, attempting a polite smile.

"Well, come on then," George commands, leading him over to a corner of the room. "Gotta meet Uncle Zeb, Nia's great-uncle," he says, bending to the sleeping elderly man in the chair behind Buzz.

"Gonna have to wake 'im up!" Russ cries.

"Sure we'll wake 'im up," George chuckles as Webb stands behind him, looking dumbly down at the old man sitting hunched over, still clutching the cane aslant across his lap, his shrunken head bowed and bobbing in his slumber, his mouth hanging open, every so often emitting a strangled sigh from deep in his chest.

"Hey! Zeb!" George cries, reaching to shake the old man's shoulder. "ZEB!" he shouts, then looks back at Webb. "He's a bit hard of hearing—eighty-six this June," he explains.

"Eighty-six!" Webb notes with a lame smile.

"Hope I look that good when I'm eighty-six!" Buzz says,

turning around in his chair to observe the awakening of Zeb.

"Zeb! Hey! Zeb!" George shouts into the old man's ear, shaking him so that his head lurches and bounces from side to side. His eyelids flutter and he compresses his lips, his jaw working actively as if he's chewing on something.

"What… what's that?" the old man whispers sleepily, blinking down at his feet with a disoriented gaze.

"I got somebody here for ya to meet," George shouts, carefully articulating each word. "The young fella who's gonna marry Nia!"

Zeb's gaze floats slowly up to encounter George, observing him skeptically, his head cocked to the side. "Nia?" he inquires faintly.

"No, no," George shouts. "The fella who's gonna marry Nia—Nia's boyfriend!"

"Oh," Zeb murmurs, his trembling hand reaching up to stroke his chin absent-mindedly. His jaw starts working again, causing the prominent network of veins at each side of his head to jump in and out at the temples. "Oh," he rasps, "Ed!"

"Mm-hm, yeah, that's fine!" George laughs, smiling over at Webb. "Webb, meet Nia's great-uncle Zeb!" he pronounces, raising his hand. "Eighty-six!"

Webb bends uneasily down to peer into the old man's face. "Hello!" he shouts self-consciously.

The old man's eyes squint determinedly behind his thick, yellow-tinged glasses. As his head cranes over on his thin, wrinkled neck, Webb notes that tiny flakes of what appear to be dried egg yolk are caked around the corners of his mouth and on his withered lips.

"Hello there!" Zeb whispers, his voice gaining strength as

he speaks. "How're y'doin', Eddie?"

Webb glances over puzzledly at George, who nods and smiles at him, shrugging his shoulders.

"I'm doing just fine, Uncle Zeb!" Webb shouts, grinning desperately.

"I'm eighty-six," Zeb announces huskily after a brief pause, his fingers moving busily along his cane.

"So I hear!" Webb notes.

"You're damn right I can hear!" the old man grumbles indignantly, frowning with a hurt expression.

"No," Webb explains quickly. "I said, 'So I hear,' Uncle Zeb!" he says, pointing to himself. The old man looks down at his feet briefly, as if in contemplation. He brings his head up slowly to encounter Webb again.

"How old are you, neighbour?" Zeb asks falteringly.

"I'm thirty-four," Webb replies.

Zeb sucks his lips in for a moment, then licks them. "Shake my hand, neighbour," he says faintly, offering him his hand tremblingly with a hint of a smile. "I'm eighty-six!"

"Sure!" Webb smiles good-naturedly, shifting his beer and reaching out to clasp the bony hand, noting its frailty and strange clamminess.

"I'm almost three times older 'n you, neighbour," Zeb observes, steadily increasing the pressure of his grip.

"Almost!" Webb replies cheerfully, attempting to pull his hand away, finding it welded in the old man's grasp.

"Not bad, eh?" Zeb mumbles, studying Webb's face intently as his fingers tighten around Webb's hand. A sharp, searing pain shoots up to Webb's elbow, and he restrains himself from shouting aloud.

"Not a bad grip, huh?" Zeb asks, staring deep into Webb's eyes. "For an eighty-six-year-old man?"

With a sudden jerk Webb pulls his hand from the hard and dry grasp. He shakes his fingers frantically in the air, the pain in them tingling and vibrating hotly. Tears begin to start in his eyes as he steps back from the old man, laughter erupting in the room around him.

"Ol' Zeb's did it again!" cries one of the voices. The old man's head slowly sinks down as he drifts back into slumber with a faint smile on his lips, opening and closing his prize thumb and forefinger positioned on his lap for display.

✿

COME ALL YE YOUNG LOVERS (III)

"SO HE SAYS, 'ARE YOU COMIN' INTO TOWN WITH ME OR not?' And I said, 'No sir, I am NOT comin' into town with you,' and he says, 'Well, why not?' and I said, 'Just because you all of a sudden wanna go into town don't mean that I suddenly wanna go into town with you, and another thing, if you're gonna spend that much time with Lloyd Brickley drinkin' after work you can just as well go marry Lloyd Brickley as pretendin' to have some kind of marriage with me. 'Whyn't you go get married to Lloyd Brickley?' That's what I said to him," says Bess Armstrong, leaning forth from her seat, addressing the other women emphatically.

As Mona sits amidst Bess's rather dubious audience, she looks at Bess Armstrong and sees superimposed over the grown mature body of Bess Armstrong the young, seven-year-old body of Bess Armstrong from the one-room schoolhouse they had both gone to out on the fifth line; sees her wiping her nose with the handkerchief as she sat in torn and patched and slightly dirty clothes, her fat, squat little body perched at the old-fashioned school desk with the seat attached to the desk itself and with the little hole at the upper right-hand corner for the ink bottle.

She sees Bess in the schoolyard at recess in the spring-time, as she cuddled her little doll with one eye and with half the hair on her head missing, as she stood with Gayle Warner, another little girl even fatter and squatter. Mona sees the other kids in a semi-circle around Bess Armstrong and Gayle Warner at the morning recess when the trunks of the trees and the uncountable multitudes of blades of green grass still shone with the morning dew—the two pudgy girls solici-tously taking care of the baby doll with one eye and half a head of hair, and the other children mocking them.

Mona herself always somehow existed between the group of children who mocked the tiny minority of untouchables in the schoolyard and the ones who were mocked by them. At times Mona walked to school with Gayle, offering companion-ship to the slow girl, who was seemingly unable to speak much. Yet a sweetness in Mona, a tenderness in her gloried in simple kindness even though they seldom exchanged words. When they did, she was never entirely sure that Gayle understood the words she was saying, and Mona for her part could only guess at the frightened murmurs that escaped the lips of Gayle as she shuffled down the gravel sideroad, by the black wire fences confining the orderly soybean fields. Mona's solicitousness to Gayle was like the care and solicitousness both Gayle and Bess showed to the tattered and oddly ghoulish doll.

Yet how was it that this kindness offered by Mona was often minimized, if not entirely negated, when the leaders of the schoolyard took it into their minds to advance upon the two girls known as Big Bess and Gooney Gayle, and began shouting these nicknames at them, ridiculing their shabby clothes and plump bodies, mocking their pathetic doll, insulting their parents and the broken-down farmhouses in which they lived, down ponderous, weed-overgrown lanes behind the veils of intersecting, grey, thorny branches of trees which seemed ugly and inhospitable and of a lower class of trees than those found elsewhere; and how was it then that Mona would often join with the other students in taunting and humiliating the two girls, herself neither entirely a part of the common mass of kids and neither entirely akin to the scapegoats and misfits.

And in her shame she recalls an instance when joining with Merna Plympton to make fun of the snot on the sleeve of Gayle's sweater when they were leaving school. She recalls Gayle looking at her reproachfully, her eyes small and pig-like, scared—yet something in the centre of them not scared at all—focusing on Mona in a way they never had before. Mona saw in those eyes the memories of a thousand walks to school, from school, the two of them—memories now denied by Mona's brazen condemnation of Gayle. And Mona knew her own eyes, even at this moment, showed Gayle the recognition of the reproach Gayle was communicating to her, showed her knowledge that even tomorrow and the day after, Mona would walk with Gayle to school, neither of them mentioning this incident—this rejection and spurning—as though it had never happened.

She knew her eyes showed this and that they pled for forgiveness for it as well, forgiveness for her weakness in needing to be aligned with the more popular, with the wide middle ground of children neither extraordinary nor deficient but proudly normal, a normality that depended on banding together to brand those beneath them as inferior, banding together to brand the spearheads of their glib normality as superior.

But the dismissive hatred would fall in an instant as her heart regained the feeling it sometimes had when they walked silently down the gravel road in autumn beneath the slow unravelling of the fire-coloured leaves of maple trees parachuting sleepily to a dusk shadowed landscape attaining its yearly peak of vibrant redness before surrendering to grey, white and black. In the silence of their marching side by side, a peaceful oneness between them in their silence as real as reality itself was communicated without words so much more than the nervous speech of the cliques of the schoolyard, the glibness utilized to elevate oneself, the slander and gossip utilized to denigrate others.

So much more of a deeper understanding was to be found in the silence of the outcasts than in the backyards and birthday parties of the accepted ones, this was true. But the fact that often governed Mona's, and most people's, lives was one that Mona could not always admit to herself: the simple virtue that the pack seemed to be moving, moving ahead, and the outcasts and the misfits were not moving. They were left behind, left for dead, or at least it seemed that way—for they were alone, and those not wanted on the voyage by the majority, having nowhere else to go, are forced to simply stay where they are, watching everyone else leave as life is composed of only the leaving and the left behind; they are always by definition abandoned and left behind—left, finally, alone.

As she grew older, Bess became less the overweight and unattractive girl who shrinks into meekness and shame; she became more emboldened with the knowledge that there were those who would want her, who would need her, if only she made her availability known to them. These wouldn't be found at church socials nor at 4-H meetings, but rather those who would be there to supply the emboldening liquid of alcohol to make her come across with the availability of all she dared to do in an even more efficient manner.

So she became more experienced in the ways of older men with hungry, furious eyes when she was not yet out of high school; she became experienced in practices which would have stunned the superficially sexually experienced and popular girls of her high school; she smoked cigarettes, fitfully hiding the habit, or attempting to, in the last year of school; and scandalizing and breaking the heart of her elderly aunt who had raised her as best she could. After high school, Bess married a Greek man in his forties who owned a restaurant, and after a year the marriage ended, though no one really knew why.

Mona turns her attention to Maxine now sitting, listening to Bess's declamations, as always somewhat taciturn, never giving in entirely to the speaker, always remaining somewhat in reserve, wryly, doubtfully. A part of Maxine must sit in at least partial judgment, for it is she who knows the real bedrock truth, she whose face may show nothing, but all the practical facts of the world swim behind those eyes—though now half-hidden by spectacles. All that can be done in the way of healing, building, fixing, feeding, mending, caring, calming can be found in those hands, though speckled with liver spots as they increasingly are, and blue-veined, and subject to the odd tremor.

For Maxine is the elder sister of Mona, and more than sister too. It is she who has been Mona's great safeguard and bulwark since the death of their mother back when they were children, Mona only seven, Maxine ten years older than that, and when their mother lay screaming with the pain all those years ago in that farmhouse, when the doctors had said they'd done all that they could do, when the morphine deadened the pain yet made her rant incomprehensibly.

It was Maxine who for Mona was the essence of reality, the steadfast sun around which her childhood orbited, for their father, almost mad with distress and grief, was a distant shadow, sitting in sullen, stoic silence by the stove, and later on, too, when they rode back from the cemetery and beyond, when Maxine married young, married Elmer, Mona watched from an upstairs window, watched them setting off on their new life in a pickup truck—Maxine's bed in the back—and then it was Mona who was left behind, left alone.

❖

And looking over to Momma Grace Simpson, she sees that portly woman sitting, listening to the monologue of Bess Armstrong as all the rest of them are, but she takes in a glance that Grace Simpson, though perhaps hearing is not truly listening as Grace's large blue eyes stare through Bess as Grace sits absently scratching at a mosquito bite on the hillock of flesh that is her upper arm.

In the impermeable opaqueness of Grace's eyes Mona can guess at the thoughts behind them, guess that Grace— even now—is not preoccupied by the idle talk of Bess or of any woman, that her singular obsession is that of helping the mentally retarded children. It certainly was well-known that Grace herself had a sister who was a bit "off," who still lived with Grace's elderly mother and would likely do so for life. Was this the reason, aside from her essential goodness, that she had such compassion for the lost and forsaken?

Grace, or as the kids called her "Momma Simpson," was the type of woman continually concerned with the welfare of others, so it seemed. She certainly did give herself to the local mentally handicapped kids' association and she even volunteered at the local old folks' home. In fact, she not only served others more than Mona did herself (who did nothing), but she also excelled and surpassed all other lifelong help-givers and volunteers. She was selfless in her dedication, so why was it that she was so unlikeable—this person who by many yardsticks could be considered a saint?

Was it because she was overweight and didn't look after her appearance, didn't seem to care what others thought of the way she looked, and so was in some subtle way an affront to all others who did worry about how they were perceived? And the fact that her unkemptness was a result of her single-minded determination to help the less fortunate—wasn't that an affront to those who lifted not a finger to help those less fortunate, who might not even recognize that such people even exist?

She was the kind who always knew what was best, it seemed, and wasn't shy about telling you so. There was always the sense when you were around her that she assumed you were under her control and were expected to obey the suggestions she had for your life. This presumptuousness on her part was something Mona always chafed under, would shrug off, and came to the conclusion—as many others did—that Momma Simpson was someone best taken in small doses.

But on the other hand maybe it is simply her basic goodness that is the real offence, in that way that it puts on trial and convicts those of lesser goodness, automatically. She is not controlled by fear or discomfort, merely a steely, unwavering resolve as solid and unyielding as the blue in her concentrated stare. She is moved by a constant energy that compels her in the name of what she perceives to be the objective fact that she is here to help the helpless; it is a job that simply needs to be done, like a farmer mending a hole in his fence, and somehow this matter-of-factness about it is annoying too— who can say whether all saints are not in some essential way unlikeable?

Nia sitting beside Martha Simmons on the couch, looks over at her aunt now in late middle-age (though seeming older), and watches her aging yet still deft fingers busily knitting, and asks, "How is it being married thirty-five years, Aunt Martha?"

Martha looks up and, orienting herself back into the world of humanity, says, "Oh—well, it's something, something you have to work on." She half-smiles at Nia, then having paid this due to social interaction, turns back to her yarn and needles, her light, wavering voice continuing on. "It doesn't always come naturally—people have their differences, of course— so what you have to remember, I think, is to be tolerant. It can't be excitement all the time—you have to be able to give in to the other person's point of view sometimes…"

As Bess Armstrong continues on, now detailing the way that the Jenkins on the third line had split up because all he ever did was lay on the couch drinking beer all the time so she upped and left him, but now he's had a heart attack and been in the hospital for three months and she hasn't come to visit once, in comes Webb.

"Pardon me for interrupting…" he says and Bess looks up and says, "Oh, loverboy!" which makes Maxine laugh.

"Nia, could I see you for a minute?" Webb asks, and as Nia moves from the couch to join Webb, Bess shouts out, "Now don't be gettin' up to somethin' nasty, you two!"

"Can we go now?" Webb asks Nia immediately as they are away from the rest of the group.

"Why?" Nia says, puzzled. "We just got here."

"I'd really like to go now," Webb says, his eyes darting over to the kitchen door, his voice hushed, nearly pleading.

"We can't go," Nia says exasperatedly and with a touch of impatience. "We have to stay a little longer—I mean, come on."

Webb looks into her eyes with an earnest searching combined with the resignation that what is so eagerly searched for will not be found. Nia brings her lips forward to touch his, and in a flash she has turned and is on her way back to the couch and the women.

Webb pushes himself back through the kitchen door. He hears and then sees Buzz as he remarks, "Oh, shit, you're tellin' me, you get some of them beefsteak tomatoes. We had some growin' in the back corner of the yard last summer—MAN, those were some good eatin'! Jesus, I used to come home from work and eat 'em, have nothin' else but them for supper! I'm not talkin' about a sandwich, but of course many a time I like those too."

"A sandwich is what I like," Daddy Jack attests. "Just gimme a toasted tomato sandwich, by God, with some butter, salt and pepper, and some mayonnaise, that's what I like."

"Sure," says Buzz, taking the opportunity to drag at his cigarette and take a swig of his beer.

"Why, I could make a meal outta just that too," Jack says. "And what ya wanna do is throw some bacon on there, too—that's a sandwich for ya!"

"Now you're talkin'!" Russ affirms, with a sharp nod of his head and a wink of his eye.

"Oh, sure, sure, no doubt about that, Jack," Buzz offers. "Nothin' I like better than a good bacon and tomato sandwich, and for that matter, I can take a tomato sandwich on its own; you can put it on toast or just plain white bread, that's good too. In fact, back when I had that job at the plant I'd often take five or six of 'em, SIX of the bastards in my lunchbox with me there in the middle of the summer when the tomatoes were really growin'. That's when the old man had his patch out back of the house—and man, he could REALLY grow 'em! Could he ever!

"But what I'm talkin' about, Jack," Buzz continues, bulldozing a little heap of cigarette ash on the tablecloth with his finger as he speaks. "What I'm talkin' about is just comin' home from work on a hot summer day, goin' out back and gettin' some beefsteak tomatoes, comin' in, washin' 'em, slicin' 'em up, throwin' 'em on a plate and drenchin' them with some vinegar and then lots o' salt and pepper, and then sittin' down and makin' a meal outta them. Man!"

Buzz grimaces, shutting his eyes and making a clicking sound with his tongue. "THAT is some good eatin'! And I'll tell ya, my youngest boy, he likes 'em too, he can't get enough of 'em! In fact," Buzz notes wryly, "he'll come in when I got 'em all sliced up, all vinegared and salted and peppered, he'll come in and he'll take all the middle slices away."

"Middle slices, what's that, Buzz?" Jack asks with an amiable smile.

"That's the, you know, the ones that ain't at either end of the tomato, where the stem is—you know, he'll come in, the little bugger, take all the good middle slices, and leave me with what we call the butt-ends! How do ya like that?" he exclaims with mock chagrin.

"The butt-ends, eh?" Russ chuckles and the other men smile.

"Well, back there when you were talkin' about takin' six sandwiches to work, that made me think on how I useta take a good goddamn of a half loaf of bread's worth of sandwiches back when I'd pull an all-nighter on the transport trucks," notes Jack.

"That right, eh, Jack?" Buzz asks.

"That'd be the size of it," Jack says, "but the sandwiches were bologna and mustard. Jesus, when I was a young guy, I couldn't get enough bologna and mustard, and I didn't have no problem at all knockin' back maybe ten or twelve of those sandwiches a night."

"Nothin' wrong with a bologna and mustard sandwich," Buzz attests.

"You're goddamned right there's nothin' wrong with it!" Daddy Jack agrees. "That was back when I was doin' them all-nighters, and there weren't no time to stop off for a meal, and I didn't wanna anyway. I had to be at a certain place at a certain time the next day and I had to make pretty good, god-damn sure I was there, come hell or high water!"

"Well now, long as you're talkin' 'bout lunchtimes on duty, hear this," George interjects, raising a pointed finger. "Now back when I was a teenager, I spent the summers, when the old man didn't need me, pickin' up the rocks on old Mr. McFinistry's farm. Bob, you remember ol' Mr. McFinistry's place?"

"Yep, I remember 'im," says Ol' Harrison.

"Well, he could work a fella pretty damn hard," George recalls. "He'd sit up there on that tractor lookin' down on ya, pullin' his wagon behind 'im, and if you missed a rock, by God, that guy'd be on your ass so fast it'd make your head spin. Anyway, I'd be what, about seventeen or eighteen, and of course when you're a young fella like that you got a pretty good appetite anyway, but after the way McFinistry worked us, with the sun beatin' down on our backs all morning, by God, I was ready to eat a horse every day, couldn't wait for noontime to come around—and of course we had to eat out there in the field without a speck of shade to sit in. But any-way, what I would take to that job would be eight big sand-wiches o' pickle and cheese—or ham if we had it, but that was rare—a couple apples, one whole thermos of coffee, another of chicken soup and half a pie!"

"Yeah!" Harley suddenly pipes up. "And sometimes when I'm out workin', I can eat a whole turkey!"

"Harley, you shut up!" Jack shouts at the snickering teenager as George looks darkly down upon him. "I'll be damned if you ever even knew what it was like to do an honest day's work in your life!" Jack fumes, and George glares at the boy furiously, before pursing his lips and shaking his head in disgust, quelling his distaste with a long draught of his beer.

"Hey, who the hell's shootin' the shit in here?" a voice rings out, and everyone turns to see a diminutive man walk in, squat, with incongruously muscled arms, shoulder-length hair and a round face with a tiny pug nose.

"Hey, well if it ain't Raymond!" George shouts out, forgetting his disgruntlement.

"Hey, Ray!" Jack calls, and the rest of the men greet the small man now striding into the room, a cigarette jutting from his smirking lips, his left arm upraised, giving the thumbs-up signal.

"Congratulations on your anniversary, George!" Raymond says, clasping George's hand and shaking it energetically.

"What'll you be havin' to drink, Ray?" George asks.

"You know me, George—I'm a bottle baby!" Raymond attests, and Jack and Harley guffaw as a beer is passed to Raymond who snaps it open and downs half of it in one grand, ostentatious gulp, then pulls the bottle from his lips and delivers himself of a long, rumbling, wrenching belch.

"Sure nothin' else came up with that one, Ray?" Buzz asks with a grin.

"Oh I'm fine, Buzz. Jesus, this is prob'ly the last thing I need, a beer, Jesus," he pauses to shake his head and pull on his cigarette, exhaling a vast cloud of smoke up to the ceiling. "I was out last night with the girlfriend, got so goddamned pie-eyed I couldn't see straight. It's a wonder I was even standin'. Somehow I got into the truck and got us home, out there on Highway 7. I don't even know how, I can't even remember how we got home. Jesus!" he says, shaking his head.

"Ah!" says Buzz dismissively, swatting Raymond's story away with his hand. "That's when ya know you've had a good night of it, if you don't know how you got home!"

At this point the room erupts in laughter, and Jack shouts out, "That's right, Buzz, that's right!"

"Sure," Buzz says. "I've had plenty a nights where I wasn't sure how I got home, but more 'n that, I couldn't remember where I'd been to get home from in the first place! Now that's what's called havin' a good time—and you can't get all bent outta shape just 'cause you can't remember exactly the way you got back, Ray."

"Yeah, yeah, I guess you're right, there, Buzz," Raymond says meditatively, looking down gravely at the floor.

"Shit," Buzz says, "my method is first thing you wake up, get outta bed and go to the window and make sure your vehicle's still in the driveway—not halfway down the road in the ditch somewhere," he says, leaning towards Raymond and whispering in a gesture of exaggerated confidentiality, "like it's been the case different times for me."

"Right, Buzz, right," agrees Raymond, puffing at his cigarette.

"Of course, the next step after that," Buzz offers, "is to

check the car for any dents or blood stains." He winks, at which point Raymond and the rest of the men chortle, Elmer weighing in with his rumbling laughter.

"How's that girlfriend of yours doin', anyhow, Ray?" George inquires

"Oh, just the same, George, just the same," Raymond replies and throws the lower half of his body into a spasmodic approximation of orgasm that sends the rest of the men into hysterics. "Yep, she's a-puttin' her out and I'm a-takin' her in!" he cries above the laughter. "The truth is," Raymond offers, "she's just like the rest of 'em—they're either buildin' ya up or they're tearin' ya down."

"Ain't that the truth!" Daddy Jack affirms.

"They only got two settings on these women," Raymond asserts, draining down the last of his beer and lighting another cigarette. "They're either bein' bitchy or bossy—and the fuckin' ya get ain't worth the fuckin' ya get!"

The men voice their approval of this latest witticism and Raymond suddenly blinks his eyes, an expression of disbelieving surprise coming over his features.

"Well—I'll be god-*damned*!" he exclaims. "I don't believe it!" and Webb at the other end of the room feels a sinking feeling drift down into the lower reaches of his stomach as Raymond's eyes, tiny and bleary yet laboriously focusing, rest definitively upon Webb standing nervously along the counter at the far end of the kitchen.

"I'll be god-DAMNED!" Raymond pronounces, his mouth curling up into an amused, increasingly satisfied grin. "If it ain't my old pal Webb! Hey! Webb!" he calls with false bonhomie, his arm reaching out to Webb. "My old buddy!

How's it hangin', pal?" He strides across the room and extends his hand to Webb.

"How are you, Raymond?" Webb says, smiling in an attempt at affability, his heart beginning to beat violently in his chest.

"Webb here's my ol' pal!" Raymond declares to the room at large. "My good buddy!" he calls out, reaching up to throw one of his muscled arms around Webb's shoulder.

"He's a phot-awww-grapher!" Harley chimes in.

"That's right! He's a goddamned good one, too, ain't ya, Webb?" Raymond says, looking up and studying Webb's flinching face with concentration. For a moment, Raymond simply stands peering up at Webb silently.

"But what's most important is that Webb here, is a goddamned good guy," pronounces Raymond. Webb looks down upon the smaller man, sees Raymond's profile from his higher perspective, and feels dread flowering out from the pit of his abdomen as Raymond's restless, aggressive geniality comes stabbing out of his body in increasingly sharp gestures and words.

"And what I wanna know," Raymond demands of the men, "what I wanna know is why this good pal of mine—and this goddamned good guy—doesn't have a drink in his hand like he deserves!"

"Well, shit, Ray," George explains. "He had a beer last time I looked."

"That's right, George," Webb assures him, lifting his beer from the counter and holding it up. "It's right here." Webb smiles.

"Ah! Bullshit!" Raymond exclaims angrily, waving his hand

and shaking his head. "Bullshit! Is that all you got, George? Is that all you got to give to Webb who's come all the way down from the big city to see us?"

"Well," George comments laconically, "there's some liquor over there on the counter. I suspect if you think he needs a better drink, you're free to mix 'im up one yourself, if you want." George grunts, raising his beer to his lips.

"Damn right I'm gonna fix somethin' special up for Webb," Raymond vows, striding purposefully over to the bottle on the counter, twisting off the cap, pulling out a glass, his cigarette dangling from his lips.

"Hey Ray," Jack calls out. "How's it workin' out over at the foundry? Heard you got on steady over there."

"Ah it's fine, it's a fuckin' job," Raymond notes, squinting his eye from the smoke of his cigarette. "What the hell, the boss is a prick, the pay's shitty. I'm workin' my balls off to make someone else rich—like I said, it's a job."

"That's it, that's it," says Buzz, now slurring a bit, his eyes narrowing as the night wears on. "Can't say no more 'n that, eh? It's a job. Same as me—I get up, go to work, come home, watch TV, sleep, same fuckin' thing day after day. I'm just like a machine, a robot. Turn over the money to the wife every Friday and what do I get? A carton of cigarettes and a case of beer a week," he observes sombrely as he studies the end of his cigarette before he brings it to his lips and takes a long drag.

"Yep, that's the drill," says Raymond, putting the finishing touches to Webb's drink. "But one thing for sure—we got a fine drink for our ol' pal Webb, here," he proclaims, holding up the glass and displaying it for all to see.

"Here ya go, Webb, drink up," he says, handing the glass

to Webb, who takes it uneasily. "Have a good drink, pal, you deserve it," Raymond insists, looking up at Webb. "Let me see ya take a good long haul on that drink I made special for ya."

Webb sips at the drink, feeling the hotness of its potency scald his throat, sending shooting sparks through his chest.

"That's no gulp!" Raymond says angrily. "What's the matter, don't ya appreciate the effort I took in makin' ya a special drink? Take a big gulp!" he orders forcefully. He remains staring up at Webb, his brow furrowed with severe disapproval. He brings his beer to his lips and sucks its last few drops with impatient fury.

"C'mon! Let me see ya haul off and take a big gulp of it!" Raymond sneers, bringing his cigarette to his lips but just holding it there without taking a drag, studying Webb with rapt attention.

With all the men in the room now absorbed in his plight, Webb brings the glass to his mouth and drains as much as he is able, his throat nearly gagging with the awful bitterness of the liquor, his mind invaded by an unpleasant, encompassing feverish fog. Tears start in his eyes as he brings his head forward and surveys the room through a sudden blur—Buzz, Harley, Jack, George, Russ, Ol' Harrison and Elmer all looking at him with detached, almost scientific interest, bereft of pity or concern—and Raymond, nearest, grins malevolently.

"Might as well finish 'er up now, Webb, why not?" he says, dragging on his cigarette now burning down to its filter, and Webb sips at the remaining liquid in the glass. "Or don't ya like me, Webb? We're good pals, eh? Don't ya think?" Raymond remarks. Webb merely stares blankly at him for a moment, frozen. "Don't ya like me, Webb? Ain't I a good pal of yours?"

Raymond asks angrily, almost hissing the words through his teeth. Webb tilts his head back, draining the remainder of the alcohol.

Raymond looks grimly over the room as a strange silence settles upon it. He pulls his cigarette pack from the back pocket of his jeans and lights one, exhaling the smoke thoughtfully as he shakes the match out.

"Nope—I don't think Webb likes me too much," he announces to the room. "Nope—I don't think ol' Webb likes me too much at all," he says almost sorrowfully, yet deeply angry that this should be the case.

"Nope," he shakes his head, frowning with consternation. "I don't think ... that Webb ... is any kind ... of a friend ... of mine." He looks down in stern contemplation of this fact, then remarks, "Fuck—I need a beer." He strides to the fridge, helps himself to a beer, then storms from the room.

After a moment, George turns to Russ and asks, "How's that new car of yours workin' out, Russ? Got 'er broken in yet?"

"Yep, we been workin' 'er pretty good, no complaints yet," Russ replies, his fingers interlocked over his sizable belly.

"And did you get the four-door or the two-door on that?" George asks.

"Well, we got the four-door," Russ explains, gesturing, painting the picture of the car in the air with his hands. "We thought of goin' with the two-door, but what with gettin' in and out, and havin' to go pick up Ernestine's mother, who as you know is gettin' old and of course could always sit in the front seat if need be when we take her to and from church each Sunday, but anyway, I think she'd be just as happy, or happier, if she sat in the back seat, so why not get the four-door and make it easier for her to get in and out of the back seat?"

"Well hell, Russ," Buzz smiles, winking mischievously over at Elmer. "You get a new car every year anyway, don't ya?"

Russ bursts into good-natured laughter. "Nope! That ain't me you're thinkin' about, Buzz!" he hoots. "That ain't my league!"

"Well you then, George, you buy a new car pretty much every year then, don't ya?" Buzz asks as Elmer chuckles gently.

"Oh no, I don't buy 'em every year, no," George coughs, looking away.

"Well, seems to me you just got a new one, and it's no more 'n a year that I bought your ol' car off you when you were gettin' a new one," Buzz insists argumentatively.

"Well shit anyway," he says wryly, shrugging. "If I had your kinda money, I'd sure be gettin' myself a new car every year too."

"Oh bullshit," George remarks, reddening somewhat as he takes a long swig of his beer.

"No! No bullshit," Buzz says emphatically, shaking his head from side to side. "No bullshit! I'd do the same god-damned thing!" he insists. "But I don't think," he says, look-ing slyly sideways at Elmer, "I'd be sellin' my old car before I fixed the shocks on 'er!"

George looks quickly, sharply at Buzz. "You're gonna bring that up again?"

Buzz drinks from his beer and smacks his lips, looking about the room. "Nope!" he says. "I ain't bringin' it up—I'm just sayin', though, I coulda had the same make of car, the same year, from a place on Indian Road in town here, for a lot lower price than what I paid you, without the extra money I had to spend gettin' the shocks replaced."

"Well then, you'd have been probably better off goin' with that deal then, wouldn't ya?" George declares angrily, his eyes blazing as he snaps at Buzz. "No one was stoppin' ya from buyin' the one here in town, were they?"

Buzz raises his palms to George, as if fending him off.

"Hey! Hey! George relax! Shit!" he says, apparently astonished by George's vehemence. "Hey! It's no problem! No problem!" he says, his eyes glinting up at George from where he sits in his chair. "You don't have to get so goddamned ugly all's I'm sayin.'"

"I know what you're sayin'!" George exclaims furiously, his face reddening, drops of saliva spraying from his lips as he speaks, his body tensing as he stands before Buzz. "And if you think I'm gonna..."

"Well—are we ready to go home now?" a female voice inquires, and at that moment everyone turns to see Mona Hendricks standing in the kitchen doorway, all alike taken by surprise as no one had been aware of her presence.

None more so than Webb, who suddenly finds himself falling against the wall he stands by for no apparent reason, and whose attention until that moment had been focused on the sight of the tiny drops of saliva spraying from George's lips as he shouted angrily at Buzz. In Webb's mind these drops of saliva had come to represent an unnameable yet infinitely overpowering and infinitely horrifying aspect of existence; the drops of saliva were but minute manifestations of an awful and awesome ugliness, which one is always in some manner conscious of on a day-to-day basis as a sinister force blighting all that could be good or uplifting in life, yet which one is able to bear on that level until the moment when one is forced to confront it, to contemplate it in all its complexities and implications, whereupon it immobilizes and repulses one to the core of one's being, literally sapping one's will to live.

A cold sweat breaks out on Webb's forehead as he stares helplessly about the room: as he sees Elmer's tired, wan face now more serious as he observes the byplay between George and Buzz; as he sees the wrinkled, morose expression of Ol' Harrison; as he sees the elderly Uncle Zeb now hunched over, his frail, veined, sickly white head—like an infant's—almost bobbing down to his lap; as he sees Buzz with his hands upraised in his *all's I'm sayin'!* gesture, his squinting, arrogant eyes, his features expressing all the contours of obsequious hostility; as he sees Daddy Jack gazing on with an amused grin frozen on his face; and as he sees, with some surprise and distress, Harley staring directly up at him, snickering with scornful glee, his lips twitching with sardonic mirth as he observes Webb once again collapse against the wall.

The pitiless contempt in Harley's eyes becomes somehow joined with the drops of saliva from George's lips, with the memory of the sound of Raymond's sneering, self-pitying voice, and Webb is overtaken by an instantaneous and awful sense of necessity as he suddenly rushes forward and jogs around the kitchen table as the whole house around him tilts like a sinking ship. He brushes past Mona in the doorway, stumbles through the screen door into the warm, still summer night, sprints into the utter blackness and with a painful yet liberating sense of relief, bends over almost double and delivers the contents of his stomach into the sightless void of the backyard night.

He stands coughing and gasping, strands of his emission still clinging to his beard as he turns, and through watery eyes looks back at the house, sees dimly through the window into the golden light of the living room, where Raymond and Nia sit in apparent deep conversation.

The window becomes another light that spirals around, dizzying him. As he looks up, the stars and the moon, too, drift and shift about the sky as he stumbles on the uneven earth, his stomach lurching, collecting itself for another purging. His ears, though muffled and encased by their ringing, suddenly discern a tinkling, trickling sound nearby, and he makes the concerted effort to turn and see a man standing with his back to him, urinating against the tire of a truck. The man zippers up, turns and strides towards Webb, heading back to the house.

"Hey pal," Buzz says, laying his hand on Webb's shoulder. "You all right, partner?" he asks. Webb, utilizing all his power to remain upright, nods mutely. "Take it easy, eh, partner?" Buzz advises, patting his back as he strides towards the house, adding, "Keep smilin', eh?" as Webb convulses in the first throes of his next upheaval.

"Well, I guess we'd best be gettin' home too," Maxine is saying as Buzz re-enters the kitchen.

Elmer rises, muttering, "Yep, I suspect so."

"Gotta do the chores in the mornin', eh, Elmer?" Buzz asks.

"Nope, no chores to do anymore, Buzz," Elmer pronounces as Maxine puts a light jacket over his shoulders and Mona emerges from Janey's room with the two boys who'd been sleeping with Janey in her bed, the two kids still sleeping yet shuffling along, half-held up by Mona's hands.

"You want to take one of them?" Mona asks her husband, and Buzz lifts the younger boy up over his shoulder like a sack of wheat.

"Well so long, happy anniversary," they say to George and Martha. "See ya later! Take it easy!" and the people begin emerging into the night.

Elmer and Maxine walk to their car, Maxine heading to the driver's side.

"You ain't drivin' anymore, Elmer?" Buzz calls out across the yard.

"Doctor don't want 'im drivin' anymore at night," Maxine says as she gets into the car, "since he lost the sight in his one eye from the stroke."

"Oh, that right, eh?" Buzz remarks as he puts his son into his back seat and gets into his car. "Well, night then."

"Night," says Maxine in a sing-song voice. "See ya later!"

"See ya later," says Mona, starting the car, and Buzz slams the door on his side. The dogs come tearing through the night to bark at the cars as they start up the laneway following the silvery-gold pathway of their headlights' gaze, each individual stone of gravel illuminated and passing swiftly out of sight as all around the large, black-purple night stretches out to infinity, not even a few pinpricks of light on the horizon, the dogs passionately barking the cars all the way up the laneway, yet giving up their pursuit a surprisingly short distance away from the property—their barks getting fainter as they reluctantly stop and simply stand barking on either side of the road, bidding their strange farewell as they fade shrinking into night, swallowed by the darkness.

❀

In the darkness of his car, Buzz lights a cigarette, exhaling disgustedly and shaking his head. "That damn George," he remarks after a moment. "He knows just as goddamn well as I do that those shocks…"

"I would appreciate it if you wouldn't purposely go around starting arguments with my family," Mona states.

At this, Buzz grimaces and turns his head jerkily to gaze out the side window, aware that he has fucked up again, messed everything up, yet angry that this should be so, as if in accordance to an agreement he'd signed long ago he's unable to experience real contrition; he can only react to the discomfort caused by his shame by getting angrier, more self-pitying. He wrestles in his heart with an impulse of almost violent hostility. In a moment, however, he is able to drag on his cigarette and stare into the night with wry, philosophical resignation.

"And that damn Elmer," Buzz remarks, clicking his tongue and shaking his head. "I guess that stroke really took somethin' out of 'im! He was lookin' awful tonight! Awful!" Buzz exclaims, gazing into the slicing light before him beyond the windshield. "Jesus! I remember when that guy was like a giant! Strong as a horse—now seems like he can hardly sit up," Buzz laments.

"Useta be he coulda drank anyone under the table—I watched him tonight and all he did all night long was nurse one beer! Shee—it!" Buzz curses scornfully, and as genuine as his angry distress is, he desires for one of these comments to gain some purchase on the icy cliff of Mona's silence as they crackle down the sideroad in the night. As no response is forthcoming, he shrugs, returning to his posture of detached resignation, peering into the night.

In his studied nonchalance comes a song he hums almost inaudibly, almost unconsciously, coming to his lips naturally as they proceed to their home through darkness. He croons quietly:

> On top of Old Smokey,
> all covered in snow
> I lost my true sweetheart
> for courting too slow…

His voice rises as he gives himself to singing the song, his hand holding his cigarette upraised and gesturing, as if conducting his own accompanying orchestra as they pass through the shadows of the night-blackened countryside, the children sleeping softly in the back seat. He croons, half-singing, half-intoning:

> For courting's a pleasure
> and parting's a grief,
> but a false-hearted lover
> is worse than a thief.

☼

DAVID CROWE

NOBODY LIKES DAVID CROWE OF THE CROWE FAMILY living in a ramshackle house in a big, weedy field—David Crowe, who was born premature thus is anemic, thus is weak and tiny with pale, weak pipe-cleaner arms.

"That boy's unhealthy," remarks Buzz with a wince of distaste.

"Hush—he was born premature," comes the cross reminder.

David Crowe the puny has dark, red freckles speckling and blotching his white clown face like drops of blood flecking and flying through the air, disturbing, like a spot of blood in an egg yolk. A grey, dull film covers his sizable teeth. He walks to school in his mother's cast-off plaid slacks. Bullies don't beat him, teachers don't try him and animals shirk from him.

"Kitty kitty kitty," David lisps, crawling underneath the

house. The kitty is no more—he can't understand why the cats keep running away.

The principal says he is very aware of David's special educational needs. The teachers say, "Yes, David. Well, David…" When David is out of the room, they say, "We must take special care to integrate David into our activities, class," and all the children laugh at David in his mother's cast-off plaid slacks and run away giggling from him at lunchtime when he comes up with pieces of Oreo cookie imbedded in the grey film of his teeth.

Yet no hand is lifted to David—there's an unspoken agreement on the playground—and at no time is he pushed backwards over the hunched form of a complicit chuckling deceiver, nor is his face washed red and stinging in the bitter painful snow, nor icicles broken over his head, nor is he slapped, pushed or pummelled. No, for what purpose is it to gather the featherless, baby starlings from their nest in the eavestrough—the tiny, pink embryo-like creatures—their beating, small hearts plainly visible pumping within their thin baby skin, to raise them up wriggling in the palm of your hand and dash them dead against the pavement? None.

Cruelty must be difficult to have its dignity, bullies forgo such small pleasures and conceive of greater intrigues to be worthy of the name at all (though when choosing teams for baseball, as a rule David is left standing all alone, the kids arguing about who'll take him—nobody wants to lose). David Crowe sits on the sidelines, swings from the swings; if an outsider comes to the school, sneers at David Crowe, pushes at him, punches him, the children give the guy the subtle, unspoken, disapproving, lukewarm shoulder of the playground, the tribal *No* until he gets the idea. A whole invisible, protective force field encloses David; that's it—he could be still in the womb—nobody really likes him, but nobody goes out of their way to hurt him either.

And sometimes you have to laugh when you see him running with a bouquet of weeds in the fall, when the tiny blow seeds blow off behind him like a million white, feathery parachutes whisking and wafting in the wind, like in a frightening dream, the thundering black chords of a piano reverberating through a long, dark tunnel, down at the distantly sighted mouth of which these soft, white, feathery seeds fall in the golden sunlight with the faint, quavering, lilting voice of a small child repeating a commonplace phrase over and over through soft, innocent lips, unknowing, all the more scary because it's innocent.

None of this, however, stops David's nose from bleeding frequently and profusely. It's just a thing he has (as Toby Norton says, "We all have our things"); what causes it no one knows; he has special permission to leave class when it starts.

A great many of the teachers, you see, not only dislike David, they despise him (see him sitting off to the side at lunch eating his apple) and the reason they despise him is not because he is weak and puny, not because his parents are poor, not because he is ugly or his nose bleeds, not just because he is dislikeable and vaguely repellent, unnerving somehow, but rather and simply because he does not realize any of these things himself, not like the other runny-nosed, poor kids with vitamin deficiencies, skinny with white blotches on their faces and arms—rickets—their sallow faces downturned, murmuring apologetically.

David delightedly studies the bugs crawling on the grass and does not recognize his ostracization—pity cannot fall evenly upon him. Thus the vast warehouses of adult resentment must come avalanching down, bitter swipes of the tongue which fly but cannot wound him in his womb; none more so than those who would show him the greatest pity, who would pat his shoulder comfortingly or bring a fruit basket to his family at Christmas, scoring special points with God. Something in David's unawareness of his own pitifulness aggravates them and annoys them.

David's father weighs two hundred and fifty pounds and doesn't work—something's wrong with his back. He sits on the couch with lint in his bellybutton and his pants creeping down off his backside showing his underwear. His eyes are glazed over and yellow and he belches every ten minutes or so like he's about to throw something up. His expression on his face all the time is like he's just been rudely awakened from a deep sleep or is just about to fall into one. He stares at people and things with the long, unquestioning, unhurried, untroubled and faintly bored gaze of one who has absolutely no expectation of any kind whatever.

His wife is five feet tall and appears twenty years older than her age—she wears thick spectacles and large plastic earrings which look like orange buttons on her ears. They sit in their house while David is at school, an old farmhouse, most every room of which is cluttered and crammed with newspapers, vast stacks of thousands of yellowing newspapers leaning against the walls, bumping against the ceiling, more stacks out on the screened-in porch, stacks even in the bathroom leaning up against the toilet. They sit in the farmhouse before a black and white television set that never gets turned off. David's mother pages through a paper, David's father scratches himself idly, all the curtains are drawn, all is dim, faded-out greyness in the middle of the afternoon, but for a thin wedge of sunlight managing to get in through the corner of a window. It strains through an opening in the curtains and lays a rectangular silver beam across the floor—a leisurely gyrating universe of a million wafting specks of dust frolics in the beam.

On Parents' Night, David's mother and father come trudging down the hall of the school, him with his big cheeks bristling with an ugly rash of whiskers, her hobbling along beside him, dragging her left foot behind her (a broken ankle that never healed properly). David rushes ahead of her holding her hand—he wants to show her the picture he drew of the bugs. She's wearing her special dress with pink flowers on it and she says, "Yes, yes, my dear boy, there'll be time enough when we get there." His father says nothing.

All the other kids and their parents whisper: "There's that David Crowe and his parents"… "There's the Crowes from the fifth line"… "Well did you ever see such a thing?"… "Really makes you wonder." And in the strange, bright, white, fluorescent lights of the classroom, dazzling and vibrating with the weirdness of places unaccustomed to being inhabited in the night, they shuffle down the rows of the tiny school desks with the children's colourful paintings crying out all around them.

The teacher talks of David's progress to his parents. David's mother nods and says, "Yes, yes," after everything the teacher says, no matter what it is. David's father merely stares at Mrs. Crowley, making her nervous. She keeps darting her eyes over to him and smiling at him after everything she says but his expression does not change, or rather it's as if he has no expression—his head just hangs there in time, the heavy lids of his eyes blinking every so often. His hair sticks up from his head like he's just been hatched out of an egg.

Ms. Crowley is upset in her mind because he won't return her smile, yet there seems nothing hostile about the man's demeanour: he just gives no indication he hears anything she's saying, that's all. *Well, he's just another dullard*, she thinks, but still it seems to her that he's looking through her and his vapid eyes are somehow examining the contents of her soul and finding them somewhat boring.

But no, it isn't that at all, she thinks, and talks more of David's spelling. Her unease is relieved somewhat when David comes up with his picture of the bugs, crawls across his mother's lap and shows it to her, beaming with excitement—"Oh yes, my dear boy there it is, well that's really something now isn't it?" Though afterwards Mrs. Crowley again becomes somewhat nonplussed with Mr. Crowe when, as he leaves the room with his family after the interview, he lets a sharp, barking fart crack out from the voluminous folds of his baggy pants just as he disappears through the doorframe. She stands a moment staring at the empty door, her mind completely blank.

☀

Later on in the teacher's lounge, she'll say, "Oh God, I finally met that Crowe boy's mother and father, unbelievable, what a pair…"

"Oh yes," says Mrs. Wertenbaker. "I had David last year, isn't the mother something else? Can't hardly weigh more than ninety pounds soaking wet."

"Well, dears," says Mr. Millgrim, reclining against a couch, "Jake was going to give me little David this year but I told him flat-out *No*. I mean why should I struggle a whole year with him holding back the rest of the class? It isn't fair for the rest of the kids, in my opinion, I mean the kid should be placed in a special school where they can look after his needs and get *on* with it."

"It was actually his father that I found the most disconcerting and weird," says Mrs. Crowley, shivering a bit. "I mean the way the man just stands staring at you like a dumb animal without a thought in his head—and the way he looks like he just rolled out of bed and doesn't give a damn about anything—gives me the creeps."

"Mm-hm. Well he hasn't turned his hand to a day's honest labour in twenty years is what I heard—gets cheques from the government, you know," Mrs. Wertenbaker says, her tiny eyes blinking behind her spectacles.

"Ladies, need I remind you," says Mr. Millgrim, folding his hands behind his head, "that when you gaze upon a man such as Mr. Crowe that you are seeing before you the shining culmination of more than one hundred years of concentrated, indiscriminate inbreeding. The man should be stuffed and put into a museum as a classic specimen of the *Hayseedis Moronicis*, he of the slack jaw and the glassy eye. I mean, *really*, the reason he stares at you like a dumb, stupid animal is because he *is* a dumb stupid animal. I should find it quite surprising if the man even realized where he *was* tonight."

"Oh, Bill," says Mrs. Wertenbaker, shaking her head and chuckling.

"No, but really," says Mrs. Crowley, "it really makes you wonder what it is that would make a man just go to seed like that." She looks vaguely down at the carpet. "It's a real shame. A pity, really."

"Oh *come on* now, Joan," says Mr. Millgrim, "People like that don't go to seed, they're *born* that way. For God's sake, the whole family as far as I'm concerned collectively forms the supreme argument for the invention of retroactive a*bor*-tion." He shifts his thin body on the couch and loosens his necktie. "It's not a matter of people letting themselves go to seed; it's a case of being overdrawn at the gene pool. It's a wonder people like that can even get themselves dressed in the morning. It's a crime that people like that are allowed to repro*duce* in the first place!" (Mr. Millgrim once thought of running off to Paris and becoming a writer—a wife and two kids took care of that.)

"Oh, now Bill, you can't say that," says Mrs. Crowley.

"Look, Joan," he says, straightening up and sitting on the couch, "I just told Jake straight out—I don't want him in my class. Why should I spend my time teaching little David to tie his shoelaces when the rest of the kids are standing around waiting to learn how to conjugate verbs? Get him out of here and put him in a school for simpletons, I told him, or what-ever the hell. Why should the other kids suffer because of him? I'm here as a *teacher*, not a babysitter."

❖

Just at that moment the door opens and a tall, beefy man in a blue uniform carrying a mop looks into the room: Mr. Morton, the custodian. "Okay, Pat," says Mr. Millgrim to him. "We'll be done here in ten minutes or so."

Mr. Morton smiles slightly and retreats from the door. He leans his mop against the wall and walks off down the hall, trudging down the clean, bright, glistening linoleum floor of the school to the door leading down to the basement, opens it, and goes skulking down a flight of dark, dingy stairs to the boiler room to cool his heels for a while where the furnace and the ventilation system clanks and whirs and the pipes drip and tremble.

He seats himself heavily in a chair and turns on the radio to hear the last part of the hockey game, reaches over and pulls a forty-ouncer of rye out from behind the fusebox and takes a big swallow. "Ahhh," says Mr. Morton. He flinches his shoulders and shakes his head in the dark bowels of the school.

He has a full head of grey, curly hair, dry like steel wool, and a big, red, mutton face, a broken nose he got when he boxed for a while. He grumbles a bit when he thinks of the teachers in the room above him—a bunch of phonies as far as he's concerned, or so he often thinks after he's had a couple of drinks. He was in the army once but it didn't work out. Now he mops floors and does general maintenance.

"Fuckin' kids," he often mumbles under his breath when a whole chattering, running, screaming flock of them come racing in all over his nice clean floors, but he always feels ashamed of himself afterwards. He sits in his chair for a long time, staring sullenly at the blank cement wall before him, as if he's expecting it to change into something else at any minute and he doesn't want to miss it—his great body hunched over like a bear's, the chair straining to contain it, his shoulders slack, little folds at the back of his thick, raw neck like the wrinkles in a tarpaulin.

He thinks of his wife's hands—his wife at home, an invalid laid up with a mysterious ailment, who hasn't been out of the house hardly for fifteen years. He thinks of her thin quavering voice coming from the next room as if out from beneath a rock: "Pat, is the furnace turned up?" And the mere memory of the voice in his mind like the frail, last strands of a spider's web clinging in the breeze after a storm is the same as hearing the voice itself, the weak trickling of it, at once fearful and persistent like a cat meowing senselessly, meek and at the same time steadfast, immutable, ridiculously insistent, pale, thin, high, faint, weak, thoroughly futile and endlessly determined, and it causes him again to burn, to rage, violently angry within.

He stares still at the cement wall, his face as if fashioned from iron, jaws clenched, welded together—enraged and also ashamed, his guts churning blackly and his dark eyes burning as if to scorch the wall; though his rage like an engine speeds into motion, the thick cloud of his shame gathers over it, invades it, sickens it, corrodes it. *Ashamed before who and why?* he asks himself, and *Mad towards what and why?* His heavy hands rest on the arms of the chair, the radio whispers unheard.

And there's a cardboard box lying on the floor underneath the toolbox by the boiler and in the cardboard box beneath the manual for the ventilation system and a couple of old scrub brushes there's a magazine and in the magazine there's a picture of a naked woman with brown hair and twinkling blue eyes—and sometimes he picks up the magazine and stares down at the woman with the carefree, pleasing, complacent smile and the twinkling blue eyes and his heart stiffens into a murderous hatred—her white, shining teeth like a quick, jolting, merciless kick to the tenderest, most private parts of himself. He despises the woman with a sharp, clean and precise beam of hatred breaking through all the smoggy confusion of his chest—for he knows that she is hard, unimaginably hard.

And later, as his back arches on the rubber mat, as he presses himself up against this hardness and a vast, airless void opens in his mind, he wonders vaguely if it is not his wife that he hates, that what he really wishes to do is to pluck out that tenuous, straining, demanding innocence, those few remaining quavering, tenacious stands gripping mindlessly to the last shreds of life, and to crush them to death forever beneath his heel at long last.

But no (and shame rolls in mingling with his rage, making him angrier and hence more shameful again, as he groans, spent) he sees with an ascending sense of frustration and almost panic that he does not, cannot, hate his wife; that his rage let loose flows towards her but then goes through her and past her, back towards something unseen; it won't stay stuck, but travels on to someplace unknown where something seems to stand mocking him, laughing at him from beyond the realm of his comprehension, some figure always lingering at the periphery of his vision who with a turn of his head, vanishes completely.

He is ashamed before it and also in awe, because it knows him completely and he is helpless; that is why he thinks of it as *the law*, with the law's hardness, like the hardness of the naked woman. It seems to judge him like the eyes of the naked woman judge him, knowing that he is helpless, yet still demanding him to do the impossible, to accept what he cannot accept—not now, for a moment, but always—every time that keening, invalid whisper comes and sends his teeth clattering and clashing together with electric sparks, every time his heart aches dully and pointlessly and his fist slams down with a stillborn thud on his thigh.

He looks up to the battered alarm clock propped up on a boiler pipe, sighs, and hoists his body up from the chair, willing it into action with an herculean effort, rubbing his eyes and pulling himself up the dingy stairs. The last, blind thoughts flitter and fall away back through the darkness of his mind as he trudges down the empty school hall, his face blank, eyes unblinking, his plump lips like a steadfast ledge, the vast, meaty muscles of his great, marble shoulders straining smoothly beneath his uniform as he walks.

He picks up the mop where he left it against the wall and steps toward the light shining from the door of the teacher's lounge. The door opens, and Mr. Millgrim and Mrs. Wertenbaker and Mrs. Crowley all come leisurely shuffling out, pulling on jackets and coats and arranging their scarves, the two women's faces upraised to Mr. Millgrim's and chuckling still at an unheard joke.

"Yes, that's what I told him," Mr. Millgrim says over the laughter and chuckling some himself as he rakishly arranges his scarf inside the collar of his overcoat, "and believe me, he *knew* what he could do if he didn't like it."

"Oh Bill," laughs Mrs. Crowley, glancing over knowingly at Mrs. Wertenbaker who bends at the waist slightly and momentarily closes her eyes as she giggles.

Mr. Millgrim, laughing, looks over and notices Mr. Morton standing holding his mop. "Well, we're all done, Pat— do your stuff!" he says brightly with a chipper wave, which at once bids Mr. Morton goodbye and dismisses him, then turns and leads the two ladies down the hall.

"I hope I can get my car started in this weather," Mrs. Wertenbaker is heard to say giddily, still chuckling as she buttons her coat.

"Well I *could* give you a lift if you're not afraid it'll turn too many heads in the neighbourhood," says Mr. Millgrim, wagging his eyebrows, and the two ladies again bubble up with merriment at his audacity as they reach the far exit.

Mr. Morton stands watching them as they fumble for their car keys at the end of the hall. As Mr. Millgrim reaches to get the door for the women, he looks up and shouts back, "Don't forget to lock up when you're done, Pat!"

"Bill!" exclaims Mrs. Crowley delightedly and the warm laughing of the ladies echoes down the hall and then fades following them through the door and outside. Mr. Morton smiles briefly in unseen response, a smile that jerks across his face for a moment as if facilitated by an electric current, then vanishes completely.

He stands staring at the closing door, the light from the

teacher's lounge falling over half his face, casting it into relief, jagged shadows eating away the other side of his features, the sockets of his eyes and the hollows of his cheeks ensconced in brooding darkness. He stands still staring at the door after they have gone, clutching his mop.

◉

In the spring a new boy comes to the school, a little stockily built young man with choppy black hair. His parents just moved into the area as a result of his dad's job being transferred from Texas. On the first day in class, Mrs. Crowley says, "Children, a new student's come to join us, Joseph Hardwick. I hope you'll all make him feel comfortable." The boy sits with his eyes wide and staring down at the edge of his desk while feeling twenty gazes laid upon him, shamelessly curious, whispering and giggling here and there.

Later during History when the students are taking turns reading paragraphs, Mrs. Crowley says, "Joseph, could you read the next part, please?" and all the kids focus upon him anew as he stumbles through the reading in his strange, southern accent, his words seeming weird and misshapen, differently coloured like exotic birds to the children's ears. They all exchange mocking glances, erupting in hushed giggles throughout the room. Becoming conscious of this, the boy pauses in his reading, swallows, and starts reading again, losing his place, stuttering over the words as a bright red patch of embarrassment and anger, round and wide as a half-dollar coin, appears on each of his cheeks. He licks his lips, his mouth straining for moisture, his eyes darting to each side, and his voice dries out, weakens into something little more than a whisper.

"Joseph!" the teacher says. "I'm afraid you'll have to start over again. We can't make out a word you're saying."

The boy looks down, pursing his lips, the red on his cheeks spreading out. "And please speak up a bit and let us hear that wonderful accent of yours—it's really quite lovely." The boy looks up at her and then turns to the book, reading boldly, loudly, his voice rising and swelling over the phrases with emphatic pride.

At recess the children flood out from the doors, across the asphalt with the hopscotch and the basketball lines painted on it, and out into the grassy schoolyard. They separate into little clots of boys and girls, and Joseph brings up the rear, the boys in their camaraderie regarding him with backward glances. They play kickball and he stands at the side looking on, his hands in his pockets, his feet tentatively scraping the ground, his stocky body small and alone and hesitating against the sky until one of them yells, "Joseph, take it!" and he runs in, kicking, racing around the field, scores. Cheers and hoorays in the merry, determined play of boys in the afternoon field, echoes of whoops and exhortations float out and fade across the grass.

And when the bell rings, all the kids are around him; as they walk in, their heads turn to him with excited smiles. Even boys ahead of him walk backwards to gaze upon him, to hear his strangely accented voice and his jokes and phrases and strange figures of speech (which they repeat amongst themselves with delight). He walks in the midst of them, his face glowing with happiness, and a little surprise as well, puzzled perhaps in the depths of his mind as he looks excitedly from face to friendly face, his white teeth shining, his eyes darting actively from side to side and around.

And the week runs on, many recesses pass, and the boys gather round the stocky boy with the close-cropped black hair and the strange accent; the instigator of all games and feats of daring. The boys strive to speak as he speaks; he is the ultimate arbiter of young, frolicking, boy behaviour; they all want him to be on their team in Gym, competing among themselves to invite him to their homes after school, looking over at him for mute approval, compliance, commiseration during long and boring classes. They pass him notes, several of the boys seeking always to bolster the belief in themselves that he is their best friend, just a bit closer and in with him than any of the others.

They turn their somewhat desperate and expectant faces toward him, thrusting past the shoulders of the others for approval. And as each recess bell rings, he walks still in the midst of them, but now no excitement or surprise is in his demeanour and his face does not swivel to take in every beaming tribute with glee. Rather, he accepts their joyful attention with ease and complacency as his due; he looks not from side to side but straight ahead with a slight, heavy-lidded squint to his eyes, as if trained upon some destination far ahead and manly, comprehensible only to himself, with a hint of disdain as they jostle about him which only excites their reverence and respect, the burning desire of each for exclusive proximity.

And in class again, the teacher now having secretly selected him as a favourite, calls on him frequently for special duties, to go down the hall and retrieve the overhead projector, to wipe the blackboard, and when he answers her with an impudence considerably more extensive than has been previously acceptable, she purses her lips and creases her brow briefly as if to say, *Really, this is stretching it a bit, Joseph*, before allowing her features to soften into a delighted grin. And even when Joseph, during one recess, leads a couple of the other boys to climb up a tree and to swing over onto the roof of the school—something strictly forbidden—Mrs. Crowley merely makes the boys stand with their faces to the wall for fifteen minutes in the hall. "And wipe that smirk off your face, Joseph Hardwick," she says as she walks away. "Your cute face won't get you out of this one."

There is something in the nature of the boy's growing prepossession and arrogance that charms the older woman; something in the cocksure swagger of him as he leads his disciples into further acts of daredevilry on the playground that moves and amuses her as she gazes out the window from her desk. Such a healthy, young spirited scrapper of a little fellow, such a handsome—well, cute's more like it—little guy with that charming accent; you can't stay mad at him for long, even though of course the discipline and order of the class must be maintained.

"And when I asked him what he was doing up on the roof, he looked up at me as if he were the most innocent, young child in the world, as if butter wouldn't melt in his mouth," she says to Mrs. Wertenbaker in the restroom.

"Well, isn't that the way it always is with these young charmers—see how early they start," says Mrs. Wertenbaker.

"Yes, I suppose he knows in his heart he can wrap anyone

around his finger just with those eyes of his, the little sneak," says Mrs. Crowley with a show of indignation to herself in the mirror.

"Oh yes, I don't suppose there's any doubt in his mind of that at all," says Mrs. Wertenbaker as she flushes and emerges from the stall, matter-of-factly adjusting her skirt and the vest over her sweater. "Every so often you get them like that," she says.

"It was all I could do to keep a straight face," says Mrs. Crowley. "Really though, I'll have to take him in hand soon, it's getting a bit much," she laughs, turning from the sink.

"Reminds me of my young Robert when he was that age," chortles Mrs. Wertenbaker, and they chuckle knowingly as they exit through the swinging door that sweeps back and forth a couple times before closing motionless in the empty washroom, their heels clicking down the hall outside.

❂

Joseph is now outside in the misty morning recess with his cohorts—it being the morn after a heavy night's rain, so that limpid puddles gleam here and there across the black asphalt, a kind of haze settles in the branches of the trees, their trunks blackened luridly, the grass vibrantly green. Joseph and his many best friends run out past where Mr. Morton stoically sweeps the back steps of the school.

"Hey! Look, Joseph!" calls one of the boys upon sighting the many dew worms laid out across the pavement. The boys run and kneel in fascination, their faces crowded over the flesh-coloured worms languidly lying in stunned sightlessness scattered over the black steaming asphalt, squirming spasmodically from time to time, having slithered from their sanctuaries but now somewhat befuddled, lost, seeming like so many amputated fingers but shining smooth with tiny, barely perceptible ridges along the sides of them, raising their heads—or is it their tails?—up questioningly every so often with great effort, then letting them fall lazily to the pavement again.

Joseph picks up one of the worms and pulls it in half with scientific detachment, lays it down again and watches the two pieces squirm around. The other boys follow suit, pulling the worms in half and watching the tiny, shiny pieces of worm slither mindlessly about.

"Look!" says Joseph, and he picks up a particularly long worm, leaps to his feet and runs with it in his outstretched hand across the asphalt to where the girls are skipping rope, one at each side and two in the middle jumping, the rope doubled over, all absorbed, until one hears the laughter of Joseph and looks up, sees him and then sees the long, curling worm dangling from his fingers.

"Get out!" she cries, dropping the rope. They all rush away, some of them screaming, and he flings the worm at them. They shrink back and flinch with a collective shiver, and here come the rest of the boys with worms—with bright, roguish leers, they whip and fling the worms through the air, the girls running yet avoiding them easily, extensively voicing their extreme repulsion, their eyes glittering with anger and amusement and even the smallest of the boys runs off with the worm outstretched, pursuing a loudly crying girl in the foggy morn, until he stops and throws it at her, then runs back to the fold, chuckling mischievously and self-satisfied, grinning with downward slanted eyes.

But Joseph now is detached and looks far off over to where the asphalt gives way to the gravel of the teachers' parking lot. He sees the boy David Crowe, who kneels looking happily down upon the worms, his eyes behind his thick spectacles hidden, his hands dancing excitedly in the air above the worms as they squirm and writhe.

A sombreness falls down across Joseph Hardwick's face and he walks slowly and deliberately from the melee he's created, striding purposefully across the schoolyard, his stocky body drawn inexorably as if on a wire across the asphalt to David Crowe. He cries as he approaches, "Hey! David likes the worms!"

The rest of the kids all laugh as they look over and see David grinning obliviously down at the worms and Joseph at his side now inquiring, "David! You like the worms?"

The boy looks up a moment dumbfounded, unseeingly at Joseph's face, then turns merrily back to the worms on the ground. The children are all now running towards the edge of the parking lot. "David, ya get those pants from your mother?" asks Joseph regarding the plaid, polyester slacks David wears, the knees of them on the gravel, his head turned down and away from Joseph.

"David—can't ya hear me?" asks the stocky boy, his lips twitching in a smirk, his eyes actively taking in the small figure, dancing with unfocused amusement, his daringness riding upon the buoyancy of the tentative laughter gathering behind him, the children crowding around at a distance, all watching with expectant fear.

"David!" says Joseph again, bending and looking into the meditative face, shifting his head around to look into the eyes of the boy. "David!" he says, placing his hand on the boy's shoulder and shaking it.

David glances down at the hand on the shoulder of his sweater with troubled eyes, his mouth slightly open; he looks up at Joseph's mocking face uncomprehendingly, the children watching with hungry silence.

Joseph looks at David's face with an ironic benevolence causing his features to sharpen and gleam, his eyebrows at the same time narrowing angrily. "Hey, David—you must like the worms," he proclaims as he pulls on the sweater, David stumbling to his feet, now panic-stricken and trying to struggle away, his sweater stretching off his torso and his arms swinging, his face contorted with quick, confused fear, his mouth open.

Joseph pushes him and David falls flailing down into the gravel, his eyeglasses spinning off into the tiny clouds of dust rising. The smaller boy lifts his head from the gravel, dirt on his chin, looking back over his shoulder at Joseph advancing relentlessly. Joseph grabs him by the collar and pulls him to his feet, his arm around the neck of the boy.

"Make 'im EAT the worms!" calls out one of the boys.

"Hey, ya wanna eat the worms?" Joseph asks, bending David's arms behind his back and marching him over to a Volkswagen car in the parking lot.

He shoves David up against the curved hood of the car, David hardly conscious enough to be frightened, his mouth gaping open as if in a dream where one can't scream, the children all around in strange silence, their eyes trained upon the spectacle, smiles frozen on their faces, one making a vague dissenting gesture.

"David!" Joseph shouts directly into the face of the boy, a husky commanding harshness rising in his voice, his one hand pinning David's thin chest to the Volkswagen, the other coming up with a tiny wriggling worm, his hard eyes feeding on David's helplessness. David uncomprehending, stricken with fear, his head swinging around convulsively—and at this point, across from the parking lot on the school's steps, Mr. Morton's head suddenly jerks up like a dog's who's heard something.

In a white flash he sees the group of children in the parking lot, the parking lot by the wire fence and the farmer's field beyond, beneath the grey morning sky, the back of Joseph's head and his shoulders and over his shoulder the shrinking paralyzed face of David wilting against the hood of the Volkswagen. In that white, flashing instant Mr. Morton's hulking body flies from the school steps, the broom standing straight up by itself magically for a moment before it tilts slowly and clatters to the pavement. Mr. Morton in his blue uniform and his meaty hand grabs Joseph by the back of his neck, jerking the boy backwards, his hands on the collar of his shirt lifting him slightly from the ground and shaking him back and forth, his eyes burning with anger, his face red.

"*Hey*! Don't you *ever*!" he shouts—shaking the boy, the boy's arms and legs dangling and jerking. "You *hear*?"

The boy gapes up with wonder and stunned disbelief into the man's red, burning, snarling face, the sudden hate-filled eyes, drops of spit flying from his mouth, the children all around backing away in awe. Mr. Morton lets the boy drop, plopping to the gravel, and turns quickly, clenching his fists and trudging back from the parking lot, breathing heavily through his nostrils. The children all stare at his sullen back as he walks away, none more astonished than Joseph reddening with shame as he sits on the gravel.

Mr. Morton treads back to the broom, trying to get his breathing regular, feeling a murderous lunge begin to catch fire in his limbs, arresting it briefly, then returning to his broom, his heart beating violently, the pinprick feelings of cold sweat breaking out at his hairline. The children all disperse cautiously in the quick silence. One retrieves David's glasses and hands them to him as the bell rings. Later that night in the old rundown farmhouse, David crawls across his mother's lap, delightedly showing her his new pictures of the bugs.

"Oh yes, there they are my boy, yes," she says as he grins happily down on them. At their side, Mr. Crowe lies on his back on the couch, his T-shirt creeping up and exposing his large belly. He gazes at the television through motionless, half-closed eyes: it's one of those nature shows, a herd of gazelles galloping across a distant plain.

HEAVEN'S GOLDEN MANSION

BUZZ STAGGERS FROM THE EXIT OF THE CLUB INTO THE
empty parking lot, his brain swishing around in his head, feet
padding on the pavement. He can't keep his eyes still; they
roll around in their sockets and send soaring visions of stars
flying and diving into his mind. He feels heavy, trapped in his
mortal body, feels his clothes clutching to him, his tongue
in his mouth lying like a sick lump, his teeth like gritty peb-
bles. He feels the blood pumping in his neck, throbbing in
his eyeballs, his nose all greasy and filled with itchy hairs and
crumbs, his every breath a labour.

Easy there, he tells himself. He stands in the empty parking lot and listens a minute: nothing but the silence of the
night. The moon shines bright—it don't care. The crickets
chirp in the weeds and from far off, the highway rumbles.
Easy there. His heart pumps away opening and closing in his

chest like a little baby's fist—all for what? To go down with all the other mortified stiffs in the graveyard. Money runs like blood through the fingers, then no more—empty hands in a casket—can't take nothin' with ya anyhow. He lurches and stumbles in the parking lot like an old ship listing, runs his hand over his sweaty brow to calm the murky commotion in his head.

Ah, fuck, his guts finely pickled by eight sweet beers, forty-five years which have manhandled and mangled the flesh into a trim and disciplined machine, soft in the middle, muscles pummelled and flattened into grim serviceability, the stringy sinews and tendons of the neck rigidified, poised, primed for action, despite the lumpy fat collecting on his belly and underneath his upper arms. The slow dissipation of resolve, the numbing of his appetite, the heart hunched into a stubbornness which has forgotten its purpose. A recalcitrant and rebellious machine but a machine nonetheless, collapsing in slow motion, creaking and shivering, sometimes a fist or a lonesome bone slashing out, a word or a cry, for though the soul's been duly salted with bitterness, the eye dulled by the metallic creed of the stoic, still an unnameable hunger won't be satisfied or stilled; in fact grows keener, sharpening its pangs upon the grindstone of each passing moment.

He stumbles about, fumbles at his fly, pulls out his penis and pisses on the tire of his truck—the hiss of it against the rubber, bubbling and dribbling down into little pools on the asphalt, a pale, white mist rising off it. He belches a short, cracking burp from deep in his sodden gut. His blinking eyes look out across the parking lot as his piss crackles below.

Mona'll be sleeping right now, he thinks, her face laying

sideways on the pillow, her eyes closed tight with little wrinkles at the sides, like she's got a toothache or trying to solve a problem of some kind. Or maybe she's in her chair in front of the TV, a blanket over her lap, her eyes blinking shut, her mouth going slack, her head slowly nodding down to slumber in the light blue rays—an audience bays phony laughter from the screen. Her ghostly, white hair against the back of the chair, greyed over the years, used to be jet black.

And the two kids shut tight in their bedrooms... The same cool breeze moving soundlessly across his face, across the parking lot, across the fields softly swaying the tall grass and the weeds, lightly flowing and touching everything yet making away with nothing; the same soft breeze sifts through the screens and ruffles the curtains of their rooms in the grey night, curls and swirls about the corners of their rooms and mingles with their sleeping sighs.

"Fuck," he slurs aloud and climbs into his truck, roars the engine and pulls out into the quiet streets, drives past the quiet houses all dark, no lights anywhere, the lawns all bare, a tricycle or a bicycle sometimes lying like a skeleton all akimbo, a tire hanging from a tree on the end of a taut rope—might as well be on the moon—every so often a guilty cat shirking around like a shadow of itself.

And what's it mean to be a man anyway? he asks himself, when even in the midst of the most mundane moments of day-to-day living, the jaw must be clenched with quick, steadfast determination to stop yourself from bursting suddenly into tears for no reason? And who will hear a man cry in the solitude of his pain, when he trudges through his days in a force field of inexplicable sullen anger, as he bears no exceptional scar nor tragedy to speak of, merely that his lot chafes him, merely that he is obstinate and disagreeable because life strikes him as such?

He turns off down the highway and motors past the bright, neon signs blinking like idiot children waving to no one, and out past the last motel, he spies at the limit of his headlight ray a familiar cloaked figure ambling on in the gravel. "Shit," he mutters to himself, and pulls the truck onto the shoulder of the road.

"Wanna ride?" he slurs, opening the passenger door, and Happy Henry runs bustling up with his suitcases.

"Yes! Yessir! Thank you, sir!" he simpers awkwardly fumbling with the cases as he clambers into the cab.

"Throw 'em in the back," commands Buzz, and Happy Henry plunks them in and settles up beside Buzz, slamming the door.

"Thank you, sir!" says Happy Henry, but Buzz just sits there driving, squinting a bit, his mouth turned down and moving a bit like he's chewing on something.

"Where ya goin'?" he asks Henry.

"Oh! To the Wigford Church," says Henry. "I can get out at the tenth line, though," and with a mechanical, robotic action, Henry's right arm delves into his overcoat pocket and comes up with one of his pamphlets.

"Perhaps you would be interested in…" Henry begins, passing the pamphlet over to Buzz.

Buzz turns quickly to him and shouts, "Put that away! If you're gonna start that bullshit ya can get out right now!" A look of shock comes over Henry's face, then like a chastened child he bows his head and replaces the tract in his coat.

"Jee-sus CHRIST!" Buzz mutters disgustedly. "What in hell, ya went through all that shit with me before," he grumbles, frowning sourly at the road. "What in hell ya tryin' to do, Henry, walkin' the roads all day and all night long, talkin' about God and heaven all the time? Nobody's interested in that shit, for Christ's sake, can't you even see that?"

"But I'm WITNESSIN', Buzz!" says Happy Henry. "For so it is written in the bible that we should spread the good news of the Lord's washin' away of all sin in the blood of the lamb, for so it is written in the last days there shall be much weepin'... an'... an' gnashing of teeth, but the Lord has over-come the world... an'... an'... taketh us up to the eternal rest of the righteous unto heaven!" Henry stutters it all out, his eyes wide in the dark truck.

"Aw, SHIT," grunts Buzz, grimacing with distaste. He drives in silence. *Ah well, he's just a half-wit*, he thinks to himself, a harmless nitwit, and Happy Henry wonders briefly in his mind why Buzz smells so strangely and seems to slur his words in such a peculiar manner. Buzz relaxes a bit and lights up a cigarette as he drives, the first gusts of the smoke into his lungs almost sickening him, making his brain lurch a bit, then fading—*Easy there*. Happy Henry at his side sits blink-ing, his rabbit lips murmuring away to himself, and finally he can resist no longer.

"An' we must simply receive Lord Jesus Christ as our saviour in order that all sins are washed away and forgiven and we may rest eternally in paradise!" he blurts, his eyeballs darting wildly from side to side, his eyebrows dancing up and down on his forehead.

"Shit," Buzz sighs to himself. "So what's in paradise, Henry, why we all wanna go to paradise, anyhow?" he asks with tired resignation.

"Oh, in paradise all is whiteness and gold and purity," replies Happy Henry. "We shall no longer weep nor hunger nor toil," he explains.

"Hm, I see," says Buzz meditatively. "And the streets up there're paved in gold, is what I heard—that true?"

"Um... um... the streets, yes, paved in gold," Henry answers, straining a bit, "and the Lord and all his angels finely arrayed."

"I see," says Buzz. "Ya say we don't toil up in heaven— where do we get our money from then?"

Happy Henry stutters a bit then closes his eyes tight, tilting his head back and pressing his hands together on his lap. "We... we get our money from the Lord," he says.

"Well," says Buzz, "if we don't hunger then we don't have to eat. What do we need money for, then?" he asks.

"Um...um..." says Henry, shutting his eyes even tighter, wrinkling his brow.

"And where in hell do we live up in heaven, Henry?" asks Buzz. "Do we all just wander around on the clouds all the time together, or do we have our own houses or what? Do we have any damn privacy at ALL?"

Happy Henry gasps, then his eyes pop open. "We all live in mansions! It is written that in my Father's house there are many mansions," he concludes proudly.

"Oh, MANsions, eh?" says Buzz. "Well, that don't sound too bad. Mansions—and what're these mansions made of, Henry? Are they made of stone or wood or what?"

"Um… um…" says Henry, rubbing his hands together worriedly.

"Well, they'd be made of gold, wouldn't they, Henry?" Buzz suggests. "If the damn streets that everybody walks on are made of gold, you'd think the bloody MANSIONS would at least be made of gold too, wouldn't ya?"

"Um… YES—in golden mansions in heaven," says Henry, nodding his head with relief. He continues nodding, whispering to himself.

"Well, that sounds pretty damn good," muses Buzz. "Mansions of gold, pretty damn good. But it seems to me that everybody's mansion must be pretty much the same up there in heaven, eh? I mean, they'd hafta be, or does some people have bigger mansions than others, or smaller, or does everyone get treated equal-like, or what?"

"Um… um… we are all equal in the eyes of the Lord!" Henry proclaims.

"Well then," says Buzz, "you're sayin' that the president or the chief of police don't maybe get a bit bigger mansion in heaven than anyone else, maybe? No? Not at all? Well how 'bout this, Henry, what if I got up in heaven and wanted to build an addition on my mansion, or wanted to put flower boxes in all the windows, would I be able to do that? Would that be allowed?"

Henry blinks his eyes in puzzlement and stares out the window.

"I can't see as how it could be," Buzz says at length. "Allowed, I mean. I mean, if everyone gets treated equal, seems like everybody'd have to live in identical mansions. Don't think I'd like that, Henry, to live in the exact same mansion as everyone else, even if it IS a gold mansion." He pauses a moment, considering the road. "I mean, if ya can't even put a friggin' FLOWER BOX on it."

Henry sits thoroughly perplexed, the bleary lights of the night smearing themselves across the windows as they whisk past. Buzz flexes his jaw with drunken smugness as he drives.

"Tell ya one thing though Henry, tell ya one thing," he says reflectively. "If what you're sayin' is true, that all ya have to do is open up yer arms and accept Jesus and all yer sins are washed away…"

"By the blood of the lamb!" interjects Henry. "Washed away and forgiven by the grace of the Lord!" he cries, leaning across the seat with fresh fervour causing his eyes to flash like pearls in the dashboard light.

"Yeah," says Buzz. "Well if that's true, that they're all washed away and forgiven, but really washed away without a speck left, as if they never happened in the first place, and all memory scrubbed out, erased… all that would really be somethin'. And really forgiven, too, as if somethin' could open wide enough in this world to honestly, heartily forgive the worst, shittiest, lowdown sin—and to forget it too, wash it away, disappeared back beyond the past." His right hand is off the wheel now, gesturing, vaguely grasping a bit in front of his face, his eyes squinting out onto the road with intense concentration. "Yeah, that would REALLY be somethin' else, no shit."

His intoxicated mind running down all the jagged cruelties seen and unseen, the murderous thoughts and intentions swept under the rug, all the little incidents of just pure, unadulterated meanness and the sinister, burning, white flames of the countless callous slaps across the face, from the cat swung around by its tail in the backyard to the pleading cry heard muffled over his shoulder as he slammed unheedingly out through the swinging screen door—his heart boiling over with an acidic guilt that only made him madder and more determined to do it—and his mind astonished because he really regretted so little.

"Oh yeah, that would be somethin', somethin' else," Buzz says, nodding grimly, pausing as he considers the idea. "'Fact, it almost wouldn't seem right, somehow. But if what you're sayin' is true, well, that'd be somethin' sensational, jus' what the doctor ordered for somethin' like me."

He looks over appraisingly at Henry. Happy Henry shifts in his seat—and is just about to burst out with how the good Lord knows we are all sinners and if only we declare this unto Him and ask Him in our hearts—when Buzz says, "'Cause ya know what I am, Henry?" He looks stoically out at the darkened countryside whizzing past and nods once, decisively, like a man facing up to hard facts and biting down on them, hard. "I'm what they call a bad bastard—the black sheep of the family. I'm a tough, old, bastard," he says solemnly and slowly.

Happy Henry blinks over at him.

"I don't care who knows it and I don't care what no one thinks," says Buzz. "Never did. I like to go out and drink and have a good time and that's what I do. I like to go out an' I like to get pissed up," he says, his voice turning a bit soft, his face taking on a solemn cast, his eyes narrowing, his head slowly nodding to confirm what he's saying.

"I got a wife and I got two kids an' I don't suspect there was ever a time I had a few minutes free when I didn't use it to go out an' get drunk, or didn't wanna use it to get drunk." His eyes dart over to Henry.

"Know what I'm sayin'? Don't sound too good, eh? 'Cause I'm a tough old bastard is what I am, an' I ain't gonna pretend, an' I ain't gonna put on any phony face for nobody—like some do—AND I can beat the Christ of anyone who's got an argument with it, all right?" he says, his voice rising, looking over at Happy Henry with an angry, wounded flash in his eyes.

Henry looks over, his brow furrowed with concern. He's worried because he doesn't like to hear so many cuss words used all at once, but his tiny worries and concerns are forgotten as the good news come bursting through them like a bright, sparkling, blue and white, excited fountain. "Yes, but Lord Jesus Christ died that your sins may be forgiven and you be washed clean white as the snow!" he pipes up.

Buzz is deeply and sullenly pissed off now, gripey and cantankerous. Henry's lisping, twittering voice annoys him.

"If only your heart is dedicated unto Him… an'… an'… washed clean by the blood of the lamb."

Buzz emanates a baleful silence. "Dedicate yer heart, eh?" he grunts after a bit, flicking his ash through the little vent window by his hand.

"Yes, and to accept Him as your Lord and personal saviour," beams Henry.

"Huh," mutters Buzz, "an' that's all it takes, eh, jus' to let him in and everything is washed clean and white and right down the drain."

"Yes!" says Henry, his mouth working like a little squirrel chewing an acorn. "To admit you are a sinner and surrender to His mercy!"

"Humph," says Buzz. "An' it don't matter what you done or how long you done it for, jus' all gets swallowed up and forgotten."

Happy Henry nods excitedly. "Yes! You simply must repent of your sins and He will heal thee and bring you into His grace!"

Buzz slowly turns this over in his mind. "Well, that sounds pretty damn good," he says gruffly, and is silent for a moment, in deep thought. "An' you're sayin' it don't matter when I come to him, you're sayin' I could do it now or tomorrow or maybe twenty years from now and he'd still hafta accept me, still hafta look upon my sins and wash 'em out an' take a hold my hand and lift me right up to heaven—that what you're sayin'?"

"Yes! Yes!" says Happy Henry. "O great is the glory of the Lord!" he cries, shivering a bit.

"An even… even… if I lived till I was ninety-five years old and I was a mean, dirty, lowdown bastard all the while—while meantime someone else lived their whole life prayin' an' goin' to church an' livin' by all the rules, never doin' a thing wrong, livin' for others and never givin' a thought to themselves while I never gave a thought to anythin' BUT myself—yer sayin' if I was ninety-five an' on my deathbed, just before I died, if I gave my heart to Jesus, right there on my deathbed the minute before I died, he'd forgive everything an' I'd go up into heaven and be saved just as much as the other guy who never did nothin' wrong at all with no difference?"

"Yes… Yes," murmurs Henry, inching on the seat over to Buzz, his trembling fingers reaching over and hesitating about an inch from Buzz's shoulder.

"Huh," says Buzz. "Well, that would be somethin'," he muses, and as Henry's heart quickens in his chest, Buzz turns to him now with a roguish grin and his upper lip curling back over his tiny, hard teeth all white. "But ya know in that case, Henry, seems to me I might as well stick it out for a while yet seein' how I can go on an' have all the fun I want an' be saved just like one who never had no fun at all—sounds like a good deal to me," he says, beaming with the cleanness of his irrefutable logic. "Yeah, think I might as well go for it for a while yet then fix it all up later, sounds damn good to me, Henry."

He grins brutishly and Henry, whose brain is now turned upside down, is struck with speechless befuddlement. "Whoops!" says Buzz. "Here's the tenth line already!" He turns off the road, halting the truck in the crunching gravel. "See ya later!" he says to Henry and waits silently as Henry moves in awkward puzzlement, climbing out of the truck and retrieving his suitcases from the back.

"See ya!" cries Buzz from the truck as it whooshes off into the night, little specks and stones of gravel sprinkling up and crackling, and Henry left by the road in his baggy pants. He blinks mindlessly as he watches Buzz's tail lights disappearing off down the road, his face completely blank. He then bends to pick up the cases and trudges off down the tenth line in his old, weaving, scissor walk. And as he walks, he begins to smile and murmur happily to himself. His pace quickens: he's going to the Wigford Church, they let him play the organ there.

NIGHTSONG

NIGHT COMES DOWN ON WIGFORD, UPON THE DESERTED
town centre that scarce seems less deserted than in daylight
hours; the grey storefronts shut up upon themselves, their
store windows reflecting nothing, the sidewalks naked, the
whole town palmed in the earth's hand and dwarfed by the
black reaches of the sky, clouds drifting over the random
stars and over the white moon, three-quarters full with pale
blue pockmarks across its face, fixed stationary as a sentinel
except for when a solitary car travels along one of the backroads navigated by absorbed parents carrying their precious,
offspring cargo in the back seat, at which point the moon
detaches itself from its watch-place and agreeably drifts over
the passing fields and behind scarecrow trees for the sake of
the wandering eyes of the too-alert child—and all around
the creek-straddled valley and the hillocks and the gulleys

and the vast patchwork quilt of the croplands unfolded and sprawled out to the mysterious dark bushlands where birds sleep unbothered by the tiniest twig snap, to the silent houses where no sound breaks for ears unawake to hear but the slow tick of a clock by the kitchen table, the stark cross-frame of the window shadowed by the grey light pouring in over the empty yard on which no eye peers, and over the fields of yellow grass uncombed by any wind, and homes so bleak and shadowed as to have been deserted for forty years, and out again to the highway where the transport truckers speed through on all-night, make-or-break hauls and coffee-wired travellers flick between stations nervously, red and white streaks of light under overpasses, on ramps and turnoffs, whooshing over the landscape, as if no one ever lived or died there, and if they did, who cares?

Onward—time to be made—and out to the rail yards where the trains ram and crash into one another like restive bulls in a pen, their wheels squealing, spraying sparks on the cinders, and far out a cow picks up its hoof from the sticky mud and lets it sink again with a liquid sucking sound, and the lights change at Barker's Corner for no one, the grit in the asphalt road twinkling, and over the fences of the yards of the townsfolk, lawn chairs sitting out waiting for the dawn to wet them, inflatable wading pools, a garden hose curled around on the lawn like a slumbering serpent, the garages, junk, piles of lumber near ramshackle shacks and makeshift contraptions of metal, unfinished projects.

Mr. Millgrim shuts his book and reaches for the light, ushering in the hour of the night when everyone sleeps, no sky so huge, no night so black that it can dwarf the immeasurable faith of the stolid sleepers who rest at last with full belief their eyes will open on a day, a life, a world, exactly alike to that which these eyes last closed on, with relief, with grief, with satisfaction and submission to sleep, hands folded over breasts or turned on the side with mouth open and snoring like a chainsaw, laughing in sleep or with arms wrapped around another warm body, legs akimbo, sleeping with expressions of grim disapproval, or a certain nonplussed quizzicality or intent concentration, as if determined to solve a problem before sunrise—and not even sleep can stop the bodies churning, their stomachs like black oceans of screeching creatures, bodies turning and straining thick brown blankets, and out of doors the night sails on, the dark air silent with nothing to echo, the leaves of the trees hanging colourless, the branches glowing ghostly and unreal in the light of a streetlamp while far off across the countryside horses stand slumbering on their feet and Happy Henry lying on a mattress on the floor by the stove smiles to himself.

He ascends a solid gold staircase and seats himself at an immense organ whose silver pipes reach far up into the glorious reaches of the sky then disappear. He lifts his fingers poised above the keyboard and murmurs happily as he turns on the mattress, and Buzz rides a bicycle down a steep hill, his son's arms around his torso riding behind him, when it becomes apparent that his son has somehow become caught in the chain of the bicycle, is being dragged down into its machinations as he starts crying.

Buzz is unable to stop the bicycle as it speeds down the hill. He turns to try and grab his son, his head darts sideways on his pillow and he moans as the night flows on over the blue- and grey-drenched countryside: the pigs in their pens in the barn are quiet, huddled and squeezed together like so many fat sacks; every so often a tired grunt or an oink sounding like a resigned fart in the dark, in the cool black maze of slanted branches and the refuge of bats floating silently on wings of leather and green-eyed cats slinking with cunning cruelty through desolate grasses, their eyes glowing guiltily, wolves and foxes, raccoons.

Mr. Crowe sits before his television set, his eyes fixed upon the screen as he reaches down and elevates his left buttock to scratch it. Empty parking lots, schoolyards, the bulbs of a neon sign for a motel hum and buzz and tiny insects and brown moths flitter around them, a young retarded girl keeps asking Momma Simpson, "Please open the door," and every time she does, the door slams closed and the girl asks her again.

Momma Simpson purses her lips, becoming a trifle annoyed, and the moon, having followed the car and seen the child home, now speedily ascends to its solitary vantage point and remains still for the rest of the night, looking down on Wigford and even out past the town over the highway and the fields, even to the lake whose waves crash upon the sand tirelessly, draining back then roaring up anew, the white and grey waves playing only to amuse themselves, and out across the father of the waves, out across the smooth surface of the water stretching out for miles, until the land is but a dimly remembered idea, a dimly seen small blot on the horizon, then no more, out on the calm lake's surface which mocks land and humanity, where no snore or sigh is ever heard, on which no foot has ever walked or building ever built or ever could be, where land (dreaming, striving, word, thought) has never even existed to be remembered, or forgotten, that still, clean, untainted, smooth, dark surface where the moon finally finds its reflection.

THEN AGAIN WHAT

MONA HENDRICKS, FORTY-FIVE, HAVING SET THE TABLE
for dinner, now stands in the kitchen after turning down the
heat to simmer on a pot of mashed potatoes, and wonders
if she should move to the phone and see if he's still at work.
No, he's left by now, but where is he? The sound of the television before which the children sit crouched on the carpet
in the next room reverberates in waves of crackling noise
behind her, and her lips tighten with anger as she shakes her
head.

I told him to call, she thinks. *I asked him to call, but then
why would he?* The reason he does this is exactly part of the
reason he doesn't call; if he called, he wouldn't have to do it
at all, that is; it's part of the whole movement, like a flow, no
call, then it's past supper time, then it's the television, then it's
time for the kids to go to bed and I wake up later and he's still

not there, then I wake up again when I hear him come stumbling in the door, out of his head.

It's all made to look like it isn't considered or thought of at all, or maybe it really isn't thought of at all, and then going to work tomorrow (well he's going to have to deal with getting through his day there, feeling the way he'll feel) and then tomorrow night after that, and all the other days—Tuesday, Wednesday, Thursday after that—like a cycle or a circle, and it all gets lost in the days; that is, you can't pick it out or point it out or mention it, or you can, but he'll just be so ugly about it, or ugly in the first place, all mad and silent at the table, just opening his mouth to bitch at the kids (especially tomorrow night, feeling the way he'll probably feel) so that you won't even want to bring it up, at least when the kids are awake— they get so upset when there's an argument or a fight and then again, what's the point?

She moves to the phone and picks it up, dials the number, lets it ring four times—*Well, what did you expect?*—she hangs up.

"It's ready," she calls to the kids.

"Okay," they say from the living room.

She moves to the stove, takes the pork chops from the frying pan, lays them on a plate covered with a paper towel and takes the potatoes off. *So it'll just be silence*, she thinks, waking up in the morning, not talking, or talking but only to say something about not forgetting to pay the hydro bill, in that way that it's obvious you're only talking because you have to, about something that can't help but be talked about, because the hydro must be paid, in that voice that you use without bending or feeling, with no hole in it for the idea that things are all right, because they're not, saying *you* like an accusation, no not like an accusation, more like a swear word, or you hope it sounds like a curse or a swear word, but it still always sounds like a bending, no matter how hard and firm and angry you try to make it, and cling to the reason it must be said.

It's always a loss somehow, acting angry and at the same time trying to remember how angry you really feel, and him all meek and quiet and nodding and saying *yes* in that way he can sometimes be when he knows he's in the wrong and'll stand for being talked to in that way, not even meek really, just seeming that way in the absence of mouthing off and getting mad because he knows he doesn't dare, oh no, he knows he doesn't dare start mouthing off and getting mad back, not with me who's got the right to be mad right now, and he knows it, so he just won't say anything, quiet over his coffee, nodding *yes* to the hydro bill and slipping off to work, and also because he'll be hungover and in no mood for any fighting or hearing me scream.

She goes to the door, "Now!" she says.

"But we just wanna watch this one th…"

"It's on the table. Get in here!" She starts dishing out the potatoes as the kids come shambling in, crawling into their chairs.

"He's not here yet?" one of them asks.

"We're starting without him," she says, but also, she thinks, also because he knows, or thinks, that it's the price he must pay, that is, just act like this a few days and everything'll be all right, after a few days of the silence and only speaking when having to, and me not smiling or laughing at any of his jokes. Well after a few days of that I'll soften and everything will be normal again and the same as it was before, and I will and it will be, all just like it's forgotten or never even happened in the first place to be forgotten, but of course it won't be forgotten even if it seems like it has been, even if it seems like it never even happened to everyone but me because I'm the only one who knows it did happen.

It's just that you get tired of being mad all the time, or acting like you are, and besides what's the point if you aren't even going to talk about it like you usually don't because you figure what's the point

So you just be mad or act like you are for a while as he pussyfoots around a bit, and sometimes you can get him to do things he usually won't, like go shopping, or get him to give you some extra money to go shopping, and he acts guilty and contrite to a certain extent for a bit, and whether he really feels that way or not I don't know, likely half the time he's just acting guilty the same way I'm acting mad, because he figures, yes, just be that way for a few days, weather the storm, and pretty soon the debt'll be cleared, just pay up until you can get her soft again, till everything's normal and fine and the same as it always was, with a clean slate till the next time he goes and does the same goddamned thing again—goddamn him—because he knows if he went and did the same thing the next night, or a couple of nights after the same week without acting guilty and going through the quietness, it would be—it would really be it—too much, the end right there, because he knows…

The kids are arguing amongst themselves as she sits down to her meal, yelling in a bristling argument which is just about to erupt into physical violence.

"Hey!" she shouts.

"He keeps puttin' his foot on me!"

"Keep your foot over by your chair."

"I wasn't doin' nothin'!"

"Just mind your own business and eat your supper!"

"I wasn't doin' nothin'!"

Oh he knows, she thinks, that that'd just be just too much, there'd be no way, and besides, because he knows that he knows he's in the wrong and that he's done wrong, I imagine that he does feel wrong and guilty and doesn't just act that way, maybe it's half and half like with me being mad, you start out mad and then you don't say anything in so many words, and then you only end up acting like you feel that way—you don't really feel it after a while, or at least I don't—to the point where you actually have to think to remember that you're angry, and sometimes even *why*; maybe it's like that with him, where he does feel bad, then keeps acting that way just to pay the price to my angriness long after he's stopped feeling bad, just to put in the right amount of time because I don't say anything, I won't say anything, because what I'm saying through my silence is: I'm not shouting at you, I am not screaming at you, I am not going to argue with you about what is right and wrong because you know what is right and wrong.

I am speaking to you through my silence of my anger, which I feel you are not worthy to hear of through my words, and not only of my anger but also and even more so of my hurt—you did not come home from work, you went out and got drunk, you did not call. I am telling you that you have hurt me, once again, and though there may be a time when I will forgive you once again, it is now too soon to tell, though there may come a time when I will forgive and speak; I wish for the present only to make the fact of my hurt known, and until then, all is broken between us, all is silence and that fact.

And he is saying, through his quietness, through his meek agreeability: yes I know I have wronged you, I know I have hurt you, and see, to show that I know this, I nod quietly, I speak softly where normally I would shout and holler; thank you for your silence, I appreciate your not bitching or yelling at me, in return I am willing to slice my power in half and leave it abandoned at your feet—see how I nod my head—I will continue to manifest this approximation of shame until such time as the fact of your hurt has been firmly established and your forgiveness is shown in speaking in a polite everyday manner. Because maybe his making the effort to act guilty is the same as feeling guilty in itself, knowing in his mind that he is guilty, that he has done wrong, or rather that he hasn't done wrong in his mind but knows that his actions have caused me pain, and he's guilty and sorry for that, not the action…

But shit, she thinks. Bullshit! He knows full well what he's doing, and has done, and at the heart of it all, the wounding fact is that he has chosen to hurt me in this way. No, it's not just a movement or a flow, like sleepwalking, like the days rolling by underwater, sitting in front of the television set, getting up and making the kids' lunches, coming home from work, sitting around the dinner table and then television again, ironing clothes, pulling in and out of the driveway, work, bills, maybe going out to a dance sometimes, family get-togethers, it's not just more of the same and something which must be accepted because there is no other choice; there is a choice, always a choice, and at the bottom of it all, in the centre of it all, all the nights and days rolling by, of acting like you're angry or not acting like you're angry for the sake of the kids, buttering a piece of bread with your stomach all knotted up inside, your lips pursed over it, is the simple burning fact that HE HAS CHOSEN TO HURT ME IN THIS WAY.

Because he can, because I can take it, because it's part of us now, like the mortgage or the kitchen counter, like the weather, something to be accepted, or not, but what then? I go, I leave, yes, that's what his silence says: *Well, leave then.* And you don't speak, and you bend, because after all, that's what it comes down to; otherwise, what's the point, you leave. And that's why you don't think, that's why you keep it going in front of your eyes or at a lower level, in the self that goes to work and washes the dishes, in the self that you use to peel potatoes or go to the bank with, that does what must be done because it must be done without wondering why or look- ing anywhere or thinking of anything beyond that, because to think would be to think of leaving, of falling down on the spot and weeping, of crying *No* and refusing to be moved, and then what after that?

After that's a blank space, a vast whiteness so big you shrink in it, you can't even conceive or imagine or foresee, so you keep it where it is, unthinkable, and straighten the tablecloth, concentrate on the furniture, the wooden leg on the kitchen chair, the wallpaper peeling at the baseboard, anything.

Because it comes down to that, you either take it or you don't, and the choice you're given is no choice at all and you can cry but crying passes, knowing you'll cry again but that'll pass too, dash the dishes to the floor but they'll just have to be cleaned up after; thank God for all the things that must be done but how killing they are somehow, till one day you get all cried out I suppose, you see them like that, the old fat ones like Bess Armstrong sitting there doing crossword puzzles in the Sunday paper or playing bingo, their big fat arms on the table and staring down all tired and determined and expecting to win as if someone owes it to them, letting themselves go with their dusty grey hair, sitting together in the Golden Grill getting the lunch special after shopping, raking over the ruins of someone else's wrecked life, all hard and grey and cried out and merciless, especially the ones in church, their wrinkled bitter pursed lips—*Oh why the hell can't he just call*—why the hell, what the hell's the matter with him, why's he have to be so goddamned selfish?

❁

The younger son nudges the older son, tilts his head towards his brother and looks at him questioningly. The older son shushes his younger brother, bidding him silently to eat his meal without further ado.

❁

Oh and I suppose if you'd wanted Bert Walmsley you could've had him—Bert not particularly good-looking but not a bad-looking man being tall, thin, well-built though, the kind you were supposed to want, easygoing, used to pick me up in his father's truck, go to the 4-H dance and what not, went to the same church, a NICE man, or boy rather, married now, runs his own business, not particularly exciting but NICE, nice but not like it was with Buzz the first night, when Buzz came to the door the first night with his black hair and the devil in his eyes, the bright glittering of him, not conventionally good-looking either but he stood there like a fact, like the floor wanted him to be there, you could have felt him there even if you were blind (where Bert could come in or leave the room and you might not know it), no mistaking it, and those big brown eyes twinkling made Bert Walmsley seem less real, like some lower race of man, no not really, but Bert you could stand in front of and know all he was or ever would be in fifteen minutes—he'd tell you as much himself, like a good horse or a pole you'd hitch your horse up to, like a chair you'd sit on and never really notice until it broke, which it never would—but Buzz, there was the devil in his eyes, and pain too, and a cockiness in them and in the swift movements of his shoulders and arms, their slicing movements when he walked, his bright, white teeth when he smiled and the funniness of him, laughing at everybody, the sharpness and smartness like nothing I'd ever known.

Bert and all the rest of them were just like ghosts, a sharpness you could cut yourself on too, believe me I knew, and it wasn't the first night but shortly after, soon enough, and it was I who wanted it, and it seemed at the time it was all I'd ever wanted, or imagined I wanted or wanted without knowing it, all I could ever want or ever would want, right there before me and within me, the hardness and the softnesses of him, the what-the-hell way of him, the danger, and from that moment on there was no choice, or rather there was a choice but my wanting undid it, went past it and left it behind, as it left Bert

Walmsley behind, unthinkable, there was only him, Buzz, or rather us, like a river narrowing into the fierce reality of what must be, it was necessary and unavoidable, and I knew it and he knew it and knows it still, knows it while he's out there getting drunk and yelling in an argument with somebody, and Dad was none too happy about it either, maybe he knew it too, maybe he saw ahead to see me here eating supper with the kids alone... no, Dad could feel the danger off Buzz and he didn't like it, no matter what Buzz did, though you can't say Buzz ever went that much out of his way to get anyone to like him, but for Dad, old grouch that he was sometimes, a boy like Bert Walmsley was more his style, even went to the same church, he couldn't see any good reason why I should give up a nice boy like Bert Walmsley, a nice safe polite one like that for some wild, sharp, smart aleck like Buzz, of course it only makes sense, old Dad out on the farm only wanted what was best, another honest, responsible, hard-worker; must've seen he was powerless to alter what was going on as anyone would've been powerless, even refused to give me away at the wedding till Buzz went out and talked to him, "Now look, we're gettin' married—you can be there if you want to or not, makes no difference to me, but she wants you to be there, and it'll hurt her a hell of a lot if you're not there and I'd like you to be there too, now, it's up to you," so he came and gave me away, going up the aisle like he was going to his own funeral, and crying afterwards, the old grouch, crying for himself and losing me, I imagine, but also for me, maybe, and the pain I'd come to, the pain he knew he couldn't protect me from.

It's a sure bet Bert Walmsley would never've caused me much pain, and he knew that too, and would it've mattered if

I'd known the amount of pain or not? Though I've said many times to myself and to him, to Maxine too, if I'd known, I never would've, of course other times I'd never say or think that, and of course there's so many things that if you knew in the first place, beforehand, what they'd come to and entail, you'd never do them, never do practically anything I guess if you knew, even be born I suppose, if you had choice in the matter.

❖

"Way to go!" says the younger brother as the older brother's glass of milk tips splashing and spreading a white, flowing pool across the tablecloth. The boy gets up, brings over a towel.

"Don't use that," she says. "Get the washcloth."

"Why don't you give him heck, Ma?" asks the younger boy.

"It was an accident," she says, looking at the elder brother sop up the milk, and then again there's always the kids and the dark, sparkling in his eyes and when we went up north that summer and camped, the rented motorboat and swimming in the lake, him so happy that day and laughing for no reason, little moments like that, and the first years after we married, a different man then, maybe I was different too, never had to wonder where he was or when he'd be home, or think how to speak or act or if to speak at all; sure we fought but not with that long-held bitterness that doesn't fade or dissipate but rather builds with every fight, till every fight is the same fight and then there's no fighting at all, or rather it's just one long silent fight, a continuing condition like a piece of furniture: always there, never totally hidden and never totally revealed, always there even in the good times.

You tread around it lightly like a sore tooth, like a sour key on the piano, always just waiting to be hit, so you can't move or speak or act quite so thoughtless and free ever again, and yes there was drinking, but not like now; it was because he liked it, where now he needs it, with an angry, sad, broken-down need, a bitter and desperate one, so deep it can't be questioned or even spoken of aloud, like a great wound somewhere in him that pulses always now and can't be stilled, only blurred, shrouded, covered up, glazed over so you only see the outline and proportion, not the real particularities and the true depth of it, and sometimes you see him lying there on the couch watching television with no expression on his face, and you know he's not seeing what's on the screen or thinking about it anymore than you are, sometimes you see him drunk and yelling hoarsely about something, his eyes all bleary and furious, the air around him white-hot with the anger coming off him in waves, or sitting there slowly passing out, not even able to keep his head from listing over to the side, his jaw hanging open, and you want to ask him *why*, even when things are good, we're both moving around the kitchen doing something like canning tomatoes, sometimes especially then, you want to go and look into his eyes and say to him, just *why*, just that, even through your fear, and what you fear of course is that there is no answer, or rather and more so, that the answer is the one you already know, the one he knows you know and that you know he knows, and that the silence of all these years is composed of, that knowing and the fear brought on by it, of speaking and saying it aloud, for to say it would really be to stop time somehow—you looking into him and him looking into you in a frozen moment sliced out of your life with a quick, clean blade.

You fear that and the unimaginable difference it'd make, and even more than that you fear it would make no difference, none at all, that it's too late for differences, everything would just turn and settle, and nothing, nothing would happen: the alarm clock would still ring the next morning, the real horror of that, and so you don't ask why, you turn back to what must be done, and after a while the impulse to ask lessens and fades, not so much that you can forget it ever happened or so that it won't come back again, no, but after a while it lessens and fades and you can think, *Well, this is bearable,* or *What did you expect, anyway?*—and of course some do have it worse, after all.

Because you can only know what you've known, not that nothing else exists; in fact, something in you can't stop imagining it, but then that's part of what you know already anyhow, part of what makes it not bearable, but makes you think it is for a while, that is, most of the time, until...

She's moving from the table to the counter with the dishes, the kids clambering from their chairs. "Bed soon," she says.

"Aw!" they respond with the familiar scornful grumbling, chasing each other out of the room.

❂

Until what? Until imagining does not satisfy anymore; the hole's too big to cover it with, so you try something else and get thrown back to it again, all the while knowing that'll be the case, so you stare across the coffee in the morning, drive to work, smile, don't smile, bend, don't bend, feeling there's something else, pretending there isn't, trying to believe things are as they are because they could not be otherwise, for after all you did not, could not, want Bert Walmsley—and because in the end, anyway, what's the point?

AN AWFUL THING

THE NIGHT THE OLD MAN DIED AND HIS SOUL LOOSENED itself from its inner confines as he sat in his easy chair and went dropping from this world like a nickel through a hole in your pocket, down into the deep, dark depths from which no one ever returns, sending a widening wave of concentric ripples through the land of the living, the telephones rang one by one in quiet households and the little yellow lamps on the night tables flicked on one by one across the county in order of kin and acquaintance. The night the old man died, raw and husky thighs started and straightened up out of their warm, cuddly blankets, sleeping arms shaken awake clutched the phones quick to the jaw, and the interrupted dreamers cried, "Aw, shit!" "What is it, Buzz?" "Aw, Elmer's dead!" "No!"

Sudden scrambling in beds everywhere as the shock, like a cool blast of electricity through their minds, rigidified them, stopping their hearts and breaths and flashing in the murky realm between their grief and disbelief, each wanting to know that they were still asleep and still dreamed but realizing this was not so. They looked over, the clock still ticked, their eyes settled on a rumpled shirt lying on the floor as real and still as death.

The night the old man died was a warm Indian summer night, the wind like an even breath through the trees. Stoplights still changed, cars and trucks still sped by on the highways, radios played, and cars even motored by on the road past his house, unaware that the old man in his easy chair leaned back, sighed, and in the next moment, lived no more. The night the old man died, he'd eaten his supper with his wife, then settled down in front of the TV. At about ten o'clock he got up to take a piss, then his wife heard him opening the front door, closing it and coming back.

"What were you doing, Elmer?" asked his wife from the couch.

Elmer said he thought he'd heard something out there then he sat back down in his easy chair and after a while—hard to say when—Elmer never heard and never saw anything ever again.

The night the old man died, his wife awoke and stood at his side shaking him and crying his name with increasing fear and pleading; a woman called out all alone in an empty house with a dead man, surrounded by all the objects and mementoes and collected reminders of a life gone by, her voice going more hollow with every call, settling into the resignation of one who cries with no expectation of being heard. The faces smiled down from their picture frames, the abandoned shoes sat unlaced on the carpet, and the shirts hung waiting like obedient soldiers in the musty, upstairs closet forever the night the old man died.

❉

"Well now, Uncle Elmer knows something we all don't know," said the little smart kid from the back seat as they drove through the bright country morning.

Mona drives silently and snuffles into a torn, soggy Kleenex periodically; she's wearing her sunglasses and as she winces in her sadness, she almost seems from the side to be smiling since the corresponding expressions of her eyes are obscured. Buzz is quiet and sober, his eyes blinking like an angry hawk's beneath his creased and jerking forehead, his mouth a straight line of solemnity. They turn and park the car in place in the procession on the leafy street, all smelling like toothpaste and shampoo and the brisk, pungent aftershave still cool and stinging on Buzz's cheeks and throat.

Checking the rearview mirror one last time to make sure every hair is in place, they climb out of the car, Mona reaching up and picking a piece of white thread from the shoulder of Buzz's jacket, and they join the other people in clusters as they make their way up the sidewalk towards the church. They all exchange grim nods and even sometimes tight and drawn smiles; everybody's a bit stiff in black and grey suits and dresses freshly ironed that morning. It's a cloaked and cloistered thing: large and bulging men who haven't worn a suit for years seem fit and ready to burst out of their collars and neckties at a moment's notice; willowy, reedy women in black dresses clutching black purses to their abdomens, wearing large eyeglasses and their hair sprayed into place so that the sunshine bounces off of it; little black and grey knots of people advancing across the green lawn to the church beneath the bright, morning sky from which the sun seems to be shining sympathetically down.

A couple of children halt their playing in the yard across the street and watch, then after a moment return to skipping rope as the people linger self-consciously before the doors of the church, exchanging meaningless pleasantries. Everybody's a bit hesitant to step into the church—husbands who haven't touched their wives in months now place a hand protectively on their backs and then with bowed heads, as if making a pilgrimage into some unknown foreign land, step up the stairs into the dark, oak vestibule of the church where a tall, lugubrious friend of the family stands in his suit greeting everybody, a dull foolish grin on his face, hair creeping from beneath the cuffs of his immaculate jacket, and all the men's aftershave mingles with the sound of the faint, rolling, organ music playing a wandering, waning refrain murmuring beneath the careful whispers of the bereaved, mixing with the dark shadowy smell of the thick, burnished wood and the bright, tickling smell of the white tissue-paper bibles and hymnals, the thin, white, eggshell wafers of communion like the soft, white, soapy smell of the hands of ministers, no dirt beneath the nails, no hair on the back, the lukewarm, almost-liquid meek pressure of the smooth, boneless fingers as they shake your hand—and another smell down beneath, something faint and strange and disquieting.

The organ music swells and rolls and whispers like a far-away ocean with no end and no beginning, like a faint yet insistent song, seeming at times to fade and plunge and die, then returning determinedly once again. People are passing down a long line, at the end of which an open casket sits propped up on a bier. Uncle Elmer's wife Maxine stands beside the casket, her hand resting on the edge of it. From a distance, you can see part of Uncle Elmer's solemn profile, part of his eye and his sunken cheek, his nose pointing straight up. People advance slowly to the casket to pay their respects, staring down at Elmer as his wife weeps and collapses against them.

Elmer just lies there, his hands folded across his chest as if he's just settled down for a moment's nap, the hands all white, the veins along the backs of them dull and hardened, his face asleep, expressionless, the flesh all flat and hanging down from each side of his head, his eyelids slapped shut, not so much seeming serene as insanely complacent, his nose jutting up like a sculpture of itself and his lips dry, his mouth a simple fold of skin, the colouring of his face bizarre, too real to be real, all drained out with artificial shadings and highlights, trussed up in collar and tie like somebody else's idea of him, his head shrunken, small, diminished and weirdly feeble, sunk and positioned for display in the shining, billowing folds of bright, blue silk.

"I heard him get up and go out to the front door," Maxine is saying. "I said, 'Elmer, what're you doing?' 'I thought there was someone out there,' he says."

Her voice comes out in small, whispery catches and sobs, her eyes all washed out and faded grey with the hours of crying, the rims around them swollen raw and red and glistening, her cheeks glimmering with the tears trickling down. She's been hit by the white blast of death in a full-force, blinding blow. She looks from her comforters down to Elmer and back again with a sorrowful lethargy, reaching across at times to adjust his tie or to fuss with his collar—old habits die hard—moving slowly and foggily with a dazed, suffering numbness which every so often is agitated into a frenzy of stunned and shocked disbelief. She grasps at the hands and the arms and the lapels of the living with a sudden, insatiable need and low, moaning sobs burst from her in a flood.

Uncle Elmer just lies there, expressionless, indifferent, and sometimes it seems that from time to time, if inspected closely, his chest beneath his white shirt rises and falls in an infinitesimal rhythm of breathing, like an optical illusion, the folds of the shirt beneath his tie seeming to tighten slightly and relax. But no—stone cold he is, and stone still, no breath in death, and even a fly comes and lands on his forehead, crawls investigatively on its tiny, spidery legs upon the almost-translucent, waxy skin of his temple, up across his brow and down to the bridge of his nose. It flits away suddenly then lands aimlessly on Elmer's cuff and gaining courage, traverses the back of his hand; it pauses on the ridge of his knuckles to rub its front feet together furtively for a moment, then buzzes mercifully away—there'll be time enough later.

And the rock hard, immovable stillness of the body of Uncle Elmer lies there as before and for all time, his stillness flows from the casket, undeniable, incomprehensible, indomitable, merciless, down the aisle past the bewildered faces of his family greeting the incoming mourners with weak and hollow attempts at amiability, some even smiling and joking a bit, so easily do they fall into the habitual rap, through the crowd seating themselves in the pews and in the chairs patiently waiting, murmuring low, coughing muted coughs, from time to time exchanging glances here and there, and then after a while simply sitting, gazing straight ahead, the women lowering their faces periodically to dab at their eyes and noses discreetly with tissues, the men staring with grim abstraction, seeming almost angry, a tight, hard, clenched-up ball of sullen sorrow folded up deep inside of them.

People amble back from the casket in pairs to their seats, some with faces collapsed in woe, with a deep, eternal sadness beyond time, others merely grim and grave, strengthening their determination, shaking their heads inwardly and silently proclaiming to themselves, "an awful thing." An elderly woman walks looking down at the floor, her mouth compressed with disappointment as though she'd never seen a corpse before nor known what death was; she leans on the arm of a man who stares ahead as if seeing nothing, seemingly more puzzled than anything else, and surprised too, his mouth slightly open, all the folds of his face fallen down and his eyes shattered, little piercing pinpoints of hard, bright pain shining from the centres of them, beyond conciliation, beyond assimilation into the daily routine of his fleshy hands, his jutting brow with white, curly hair blooming with incongruous boyish vanity atop the expanse of his forehead.

And suddenly, now from the casket where Aunt Maxine fusses and frets with her husband, comes Buzz in a quickening walk, his back bent slightly and his hand over his nose and mouth as if suppressing a sneeze. His eyes wide with sudden, astonished grief, he rushes past the pews and the neatly assembled rows of chairs to the doors of the restroom in the basement of the church. Some turn where they're seated and gaze after him.

✿

After a while the organ music fades out. Aunt Maxine is led by her daughter and son-in-law to sit off by the side of the bier and down alongside the far wall. A thin man comes, slouching slightly as he walks, his head bent purposefully down, his movements swift yet somewhat constrained by a painful timidity. He comes hesitatingly up to the pulpit and looks peremptorily out over the assembled mourners—from a distance, his head seems ridiculously small for his body.

He darts his eyes down as he extracts a pair of spectacles from the pocket of his jacket; placing them on his face, he looks out again upon the crowd. A carefully trimmed, triangular beard, chestnut brown and prickly, covers his pointed chin, and a thin web of painstakingly combed-over strands of brown hair lies stretches over the peak of his tall and balding forehead. The studied solemnity of his demeanour as he reaches forth and lays a slender hand on each side of the pulpit somehow intensifies the seeming smallness of his head and its insect-like appearance.

A curtain is drawn behind him over the sight of Elmer's casket. He draws from the inside pocket of his jacket a few pieces of paper that he unfolds on the pulpit before him. In the sudden silence of the church, he studies the pages for a moment and wets his lips. He looks up tentatively to his audience, breathes in deeply, and intones. "I did not know

Elmer Huxley," he pauses and stares down at the paper. "My colleague, Reverend Palmer, knew Elmer Huxley and knew Elmer Huxley well. Unfortunately, Reverend Palmer had a prior engagement this afternoon and could not be with us today. He sends his deepest regrets to Elmer's family and friends." The minister nods slightly in the direction of Maxine and her family at the side.

"No, I did not know Elmer Huxley," he proclaims, his voice sounding irresolute and watery, yet gaining timbre, as if daring itself to be more commanding and definitive with each successive statement. "But from what I've been given to understand from Reverend Palmer, and from Elmer's beloved wife Maxine,"—he gazes over to Maxine now, staring dumbly before her, her daughter and son-in-law at each side staring solicitously at her and grasping her hands—"I know that Elmer Huxley was a decent, hard-working, God-loving man. We all know this. We all have our special memories of Elmer and the good work he did when he was with us. Perhaps what we remember most about Elmer, and what we will miss most about him, is just this aspect of his character: that when there was work to be done, when a helping hand was needed, when the call for assistance was sounded, Elmer Huxley did not step back into the shadows and wait silently for someone else to intervene, as so many of us might be tempted to do. No, Elmer was there. When Elmer Huxley saw that someone was in trouble and needed assistance, needed help, help that was within his power to give, he gave it, and when he saw that there was something that needed to be done, he did it, simply and unstintingly, with no thought of reward or the praise of others. We see this in the high profile

Elmer Huxley maintained in his community, in his lifelong membership and involvement with the Lion's Club, the Oddfellows, the Shankton County Fair Committee, the Shankton County Legion Club, the Wigford Memorial Society and of course here at the Wigford Baptist Church where his many years of deep commitment and unswerving devotion stood as a shining example to us all. It is written in the thirteenth verse of the first book of Corinthians, 'Though I speak with the tongues of men and angels and have not charity, I am become as sounding brass, or a tinkling cymbal.'"

The minister pauses and looks pointedly out through his spectacles, his eyebrows arching. "My friends," he continues, "Elmer Huxley was no tinkling cymbal. Elmer Huxley knew that to live the good life is to do the good work, to give so that the left hand knows not what the right hand is doing, to give and to give until one can give no more, and after that to find a way, somehow, that one can give more. Elmer Huxley was truly a grateful and willing servant of the Lord."

People weep and blow their noses into Kleenexes. Buzz slips in and takes his seat beside his wife.

"No, Elmer Huxley was not an important man in the eyes of the world, at any rate. The news of his passing will not figure in headlines nor on the covers of magazines. Elmer Huxley was not a famous man nor even a very powerful man, but Elmer Huxley did his work in life the best way he knew how. With his dearly beloved wife Maxine, he raised three children—Marlene, Jasper and Richard—to adulthood with a love and kindness that will long be remembered by them."

The sobbing gains in intensity; husbands reach their arms around the shoulders of their shuddering wives; and Aunt

Maxine still looks numbly, dumbly before her. The minister steps back from the pulpit a bit, his eyes gazing meditatively past the mourners.

"Now, when an event of this nature occurs, in the torturous aftermath of the loss of a loved one, many of us may be tempted in our grief and our puzzlement to raise our eyes up to the heavens and ask, *Why, Lord?* Yes, many of us feeling a pain, an extreme emptiness and desolation deep in our hearts that would seem to have no possible consolation, many of us may shake our fists in our sorrow, possibly with a great deal of anger too, and turn our eyes upwards and ask beseechingly, demandingly, *Lord, WHY?*" He raises an open palm and looks about, his small eyes behind his spectacles blinking painfully, the corners of his mouth drooping sadly.

"Not because we anticipate a logical, sensible reply to our question, for what answer could there be that could make sense to us now in our grief, that could convince us in our hearts that this is a good and right and appropriate thing? And what answer could there be, my friends, that would satisfy us that we could possibly comprehend? No, we ask not that we desire our grief or our sorrow to be washed away or nullified, we ask simply because we hunger for a sign from God, an indication to assure us that He sees us in our sadness and will give us a sign, a word, some sustenance to strengthen us in this our time of extreme need, in this our time of loss.

"And where is this sign? And where do we find this sustenance? My friends, it is found in the word of God Himself, in the good news that he sent His only begotten son to deliver to us, the news that he who apprehends His word and lives

by it, is born again into His spirit—need not fear death—
and that his loved ones, we who remain, need not grieve nor
pity the deceased for is it not written, my friends, that 'He
who believes in Me shall have life everlasting'? Is it not said
that the righteous shall sit at the right hand of the Lord? My
friends, it is not we who should grieve for Elmer Huxley, but
it is Elmer Huxley who now undoubtedly grieves for us." His
voice picks up speed now, moving with certainty and grace,
its wheels stumbling and clattering into their proper furrows,
now racing along smoothly and cleanly.

"Yes, Elmer Huxley, having accepted the word of God and
been born again, having done the will of the Lord in this life
and on this earth, undoubtedly HAS at this moment been
brought into that place where there is no toil nor weeping,
far from us here with our tears and our wringing of hands,
our doubts and our uncertainties and our anger. Elmer Huxley HAS met the Lord he loved so deeply in this lifetime and
HAS gazed down upon us here and seen clearly what we now
perceive so dimly—that there IS no death for one who lives
in the Lord, that the will and the way of the Lord is good and
just, that for the righteous there is only life and more life." The
minister pauses and draws back from the pulpit, gazing out
at the hushed mass with a cunning searchfulness, wetting his
lips briefly.

"We are gathered here today not to commemorate a
death, but to celebrate the life of Elmer Huxley, to express
our thankfulness for the gift of his character which was given
to us and the privilege of his presence in our lives. And so, to
Elmer, we do not say farewell," he says, turning to the curtain
drawn over the coffin and gesturing with an open palm. "We

merely say: until we meet again." His hand drops and he turns back to the crowd.

Seeming somewhat surprised himself at the sudden stoppage of his voice, he starts to remove his spectacles, but then evidently thinking better of it, he stops and gathers his papers from the pulpit. His eyes dart about embarrassedly as he places them in his pocket and steps jerkily away, bowing his head slightly as if navigating a low door frame. He walks back down alongside the far wall of the church as unimposingly as possible. The back of his head, particularly where his hair flattens down at the nape of his neck, seems to visibly tingle with shame and self-effacement as he walks away.

For a moment, all is silent in the church—just the occasional liquid sniffing of noses, the shuffling of tissues, the creaking of pews here and there with restive expectation. And to the pulpit comes a stout, middle-aged man, uncomfortable in his suit—Bruce, Elmer's son-in-law. He holds an open bible at his chest, right at the point where his belly strains out, ballooning his white shirt. He stands staring down at the pages of the open bible for a moment, seeming like a guilty, oversized schoolboy come to pay penance for a recess misdeed. His mouth works nervously with a slight chewing motion; his hands quiver with a faintly discernible tremor. He clears his throat painfully and exhales a long, sighing breath through his nostrils.

"The Lord..." he says, barely in a whisper; he swallows and his eyes dart up nervously. "The Lord is my shepherd..." he intones with difficulty, his eyes blinking jerkily down at the bible. "I shall not want, He maketh..."

He pauses a moment to squint at the words. "He maketh

me to lie down in green pastures... He leadeth me... beside the still waters..."

Bruce's voice struggles shakily from his throat. He shifts his considerable weight and braces his legs as if preparing to pull the words out of himself by sheer force. "He... restoreth my soul... He leadeth me in the paths of righteousness of His name's sake..."

His voice is a sad sigh, pale and cloudy, darkened and dampened like rain-soaked wood; his lips compress and his breath comes quickly through his nostrils in an aborted sob.

"Yea, though I walk through the valley of the shadow of death, I will fear no evil; thy rod and thy staff they comfort me," he murmurs, swallowing, his eyes staring down dimly, his great body seeming suddenly hunched and small. "Thou preparest a table for me in the presence of mine enemies..." and his voice catches and breaks like a tired, old, dry branch, creaking up into a tiny helpless cry. He shakes his head and purses his lips with determination.

"Thou anointest my head with oil; my cup runneth over," and now his chest heaves and shakes, his words tumble out in a jagged rush as the tears roll down his cheeks trailing long, thin, gleaming streaks. "Surely goodness and mercy shall follow me all the days of my life!" he cries, gasping, wincing as if in physical pain. "And I shall dwell in the house of the Lord forever!" He gulps, his voice trailing off into an anguished whisper.

He backs away from the pulpit, closing the bible, weeping helplessly and shaking his head from side to side. One of his large hands awkwardly fumbles as he tries to wipe his eyes behind his glasses with his fingers as he walks away, back to where his wife and Aunt Maxine sit, both now sobbing with heads bowed. Bruce sits down beside them and surrenders completely, bent over with his elbows on his knees and his one hand clasped to his forehead, the other carelessly holding the bible upside down, his mouth gaping open in a large, black O of desolation, and at that moment the curtain is drawn back.

Upon the bier the coffin sits now with its lid closed, its secret concealed. The coffin sits shining and unblemished and clean, gleaming brilliantly, shamelessly; and all eyes focus on the yellowish brown, smooth, polished wood of the coffin, knowing that within lies Uncle Elmer—his head, his nostrils and his lips—never to be seen again. Everyone pictures him in the darkness of the coffin as the drifting, narcotic fog of the faint organ music insinuates itself coyly, wandering and rolling in and slowly laying claim to the situation as it stretches itself complacently across the floor.

The mourners arise as six young gentlemen stride solemnly up to the coffin and take the positions earlier displayed to them by the anxious, hand-wringing undertaker. They clasp the handles and lift the coffin, transporting it slowly and gracefully from the bier. They remove it with militaristic skill; it floats in the midst of them, down the aisle out the doors of the church. The mourners collect themselves and glumly walk with heads bowed following the coffin out. No one now amiably smiles in greeting or falls into friendly, joking small talk by way of commiseration. In fact, they do not look at each other at all; they are each turned in upon themselves in solitary meditation, their faces drained and sallow, their eyes wide and unblinking as if they've had more shoved into them than they've had time to digest or discern.

Even the most pious of them seem shaken, chastened and almost ashamed, as if caught in the midst of some frivolous, hilarious revelry but now brought low to consider the most serious, weighty and unhumourous thing of all. They step out from the church just as a fine, misty rain begins spattering from the sky now darkening over, crowding up with grey and purplish clouds as a sudden summer storm sets in. The air is close and warm as breath as the people step down the sidewalk to their cars, hardly noticing the quick, cold drops speckling down on them.

The undertaker, with a flourish, pops open a big, black umbrella over Aunt Maxine as she's led to her car. Automobiles hum into motion all at once, motors run restively, and the cordon pulls out into the street in unison; the long line crawls up and around the corner as the rain intensifies, windshield wipers click on, squeaking and beating the silver beads of rain as it comes down in long, graceful needles upon the hoods of the cars. The windows fog—and wiping the grey, collected mist from the glass, you can see out across the fields as the line moves down the highway; see the ditches and the weeds as they pass by, the old, grey, stumpish fence posts and the rusty wires dividing the farms, the old homesteads with the peaked roofs and chimneys, the verandas and sun porches and weathervanes and piano-windows, and the pickup trucks parked on the front lawns.

You can see the new, modest homes with aluminum siding, but mostly it's the fields, vast and green, drifting back to the dimly seen horizon where the forests sit, black and grey, hazy, peaceful battalions never advancing or retreating, with the angelic cows standing still as statues, one here and there lifting up a lazy head to peer with sudden piercing concentration at the passing procession, then letting it fall as quickly without curiosity.

Trucks and cars, and even an unprotected guy on a tractor, all pull over to the side of the road in the rain out of respect as the cordon slowly crawls across the countryside, the landscape passing by as a foggy, grey dream, the rain blackening the trunks of the trees and beating a bright, bitter greenness back into the grass and the leaves of the trees, lancing down madly like a million arrows into the muddy creeks beneath the bridges, dancing and splattering with white sparks upon the highway before the line of cars as it inches reverently along, slowly rolling into the town of Wigford, past the old granary and the big water tank up on its stilts, over the hump of the railroad crossing, Bickerman's Lumberyard, the bank, the drug store, the shoe store...

The rain bubbles on the sidewalk, splashes in the gutters. An elderly gentleman comes out of the drug store with a parcel, stands staring at the cordon as it passes him by, clutching his parcel, rain pattering down and dripping off his hat.

...IGA Grocery and Hank's Restaurant...

The man and woman in white aprons behind the glaze of the bleary, drenched window stand by the cash register and watch the procession pass.

...the seesaw and the swings dangling in the little playground, Wigford Variety and Sundries, Joe's Garage, Massey-Ferguson...

And the procession turns and snakes around the corner, up the side street, past the little yards and houses of the town, to the gates of the cemetery at the end of the street.

The cars enter and park among the grassy knolls, all festooned with tombstones and memorials. The people crawl out of the cars, bending their heads and hunching their shoulders a bit beneath the rain as they stride in pairs and in clusters amongst and around the slanting tombstones and the waist-high monuments of the graveyard. Like pilgrims in a new and unexplored country, they make their way over to where the coffin is being removed ritualistically from the hearse and placed carefully upon the rubber straps stretched across the freshly dug grave. All come to stand at the side of the grave in an amorphous black and grey cluster, all staring down at the coffin with the rain now beating down against its lid, bubbling and beading, and Aunt Maxine beneath the undertaker's black umbrella holds a bouquet of red roses. She stands gasping down at the coffin, her eyes wide with shock and disbelief, her sobs shaking her as they catch in her throat causing her to make a constant, liquid, moaning sound, barely audible, as her sons and her daughter at either side of her hold her supported by the arms, their faces grim and tortured. She detaches herself from their support and leans slightly toward the grave, bending slowly in the rain with everyone watching her cautiously as with frail determination, her trembling, age-spotted hands lay the bouquet of bright red roses on the lid of the coffin.

She draws back and straightens, back into the solace of her family. Her eyes take in the coffin with one long, last, despairing look, and she turns away, her hand over her mouth. Her sons and daughter hold her and they begin to move away.

All the people begin dispersing slowly, walking away from the grave silently beneath the sheets of rain now gaining velocity. The wind starts gusting, causing the neckties of the men to flicker back over their shoulders, brushing the dampened clumps of hair back across their foreheads, rustling the skirts of the women and the drenched petals of the roses. The people separate into groups and pairs and return to their cars; elderly women solicitously aided as they bow and step into the automobiles, car doors slam and motors start again. They pull out slowly and inch down the little lane of the cemetery, and looking back through the fog on the rear window, you can see the lonely coffin left behind lying on the grassy knoll, the rain driving down on it.

Later on, back at Elmer's house, Buzz will step into the workshop in the garage, pick up the pieces of wood lying with the hammer and screwdrivers on the table. "Looks like Elmer was gettin' ready to put new shutters on," he'll say. "Won't get 'round to doin' it now, I guess."

The coffin shrinks away slowly beneath the heavy, grey and purple sky, fading back dimly, seen through the foggy window and the stark sheets of rain slashing down, and just as it recedes, almost disappearing from sight, a silent gust comes up and the bouquet of roses tumbles violently from its lid, turns end over end and falls to rest on the ground beside the coffin, motionless, almost as if…

But, no. The coffin shrinks away. A man in overalls comes loping from the far end of the cemetery towards the grave, and the past becomes the dream it always was.

❂   ❂   ❂

PHOTO CREDIT: AVA HARNESS

ABOUT THE AUTHOR

KYP HARNESS IS A CRITICALLY ACCLAIMED SINGER-songwriter who has written and recorded 200 songs on over a dozen independent recordings. He is also the author of two non-fiction books on Laurel & Hardy and Charlie Chaplin, and is the creator of the web comic *Mortimer the Slug*. *Wigford Rememberies* is his debut novel. He lives in Toronto.

www.kypharness.net